Waite on the Ripper (The Celestial Wars Book One) Revised Edition Copy

A Modern Supernatural Fantasy Thriller

John Campbell

The Creative Now

Contents

Prologue

Austin is as deep in the heart of Texas as you can get—but north Austin and south Austin, separated only by the width of the Colorado River, are worlds apart. My name is Harmon Waite, and I'm a homegrown private detective born and raised here. I'm familiar with and comfortable around the musicians, students, street people, and the never-grown-up, half-burnt-out hippies who comprise the color and show of old Austin—that never-ending party starts at 6th Street, then jiggles and jaggles its way south.

I also routinely rub shoulders with the geek side of the city. From downtown going north, the white-collar graduates of UT work for tech powerhouses or spin financial webs of wonder, supporting the business of Texas in this weird state capital of a city.

I used to play football for the University of Texas. Quick and with a good sense of the game, pro scouts told me I could be one of the few who made it, but my six-foot-one frame with its two hundred pounds of rangy muscle couldn't keep me from getting hurt my junior year. During the bowl game too, damn it. Made for a good highlight reel—but I was left moping around my off-campus apartment, waiting for the cracks in my spine to heal.

Bored, I made the mistake of leaving the boob tube playing in the background. An hour's worth of daily drama repeated twenty-four times, the new news channel CNN got into my young head. Once ambulatory again, I signed on with the Army Rangers. In the eighties, the U.S. played policeman to the world, so I spent my next six years troubleshooting brush fires in banana republics or helping start small wars on Caribbean islands.

I'd majored in journalism at UT but came out of the service too burnt out to work for the *Statesman* and too cynical to do freebies for the *Observer*. Moved to take a less-traveled road, after studying for a Texas Private Investigator's license, in 1985, in the heat of August, I opened my one-man detective agency.

While I was off playing army man, Molly O'Sullivan, my best friend from college, became the first female investigator on the Austin police force. Molly would routinely drop by, look my place over, and tell me I was crazy, but every so often, she managed to slide someone my way who needed help. Although my motley roster of clients didn't include many of the type folk I'd hoped to assist, every so often I made a difference. That was enough to keep me coming to the office, even on days when all I had to work on were a couple old paperbacks, so dog-eared I kept them in the desk drawer.

One of my few profitable jobs allowed me to put a down payment on a little red brick house off 38th. It was an established neighborhood, so the trees weren't scrawny, which made for pleasant post-dinner strolls. I was home working on some zzz's early one Sunday morning when my bedside phone started ringing and wouldn't stop. I finally sat up, fumbled the receiver to my ear, and grumbled something unintelligible.

Molly was on the other end. I could hear a faint sound of sirens, so she was probably at a sidewalk phone booth. I stared at the receiver, my tired brain gnawing on that bit of trivia, then realized Molly was repeating my name in increasingly surly tones. She finally snapped me awake by telling me she was at Threadgill's, and I needed to get my ass over to her murder scene double-quick. And no, it was not a request.

I didn't even think to argue, just grunted assent and hung up the phone. After all, it was Molly, and the address was up the street. With my fiery friend, it's usually less effort to go along to get along. She's a 5'4" bundle of Irish determination. I, for one, believe she's lucky not to have been born in Ireland—the IRA or some other liberation army would have gotten her killed for sure. Back in college, some of our strangest adventures occurred precisely because she's a red-headed provocateur.

I performed rudimentary ablutions, grabbed a green flannel shirt out of the closet, threw on a pair of old jeans hanging over a chair, and sleepily struggled with my well-scuffed but exceedingly comfortable cowboy boots. I grabbed my old brown bomber jacket on the way out the door.

Chapter 1 – The Murder of Jenny Summers

It was a few minutes before seven—daylight still a promise on the horizon of what looked to become a November day chilled by rain. I wheeled my aging BMW convertible out onto North Lamar. A few minutes later, a throng of flashing lights hove into view, clustered under the Threadgill's sign on the west side of the boulevard. Threadgill's is one of my favorite food joints, but it was hunkered down and lonely looking so long before the lunchtime crowd.

Brief thoughts of good food and hot coffee went right out of mind as I pulled into the parking lot. In fact, I lost all appetite as I caught my first taste of a very evil vibe. It hung over a half-height, beat-up army-green dumpster squatting like a fat toad behind the restaurant.

I couldn't just sit there; the wrongness I felt demanded witness. Unlimbering out of my beamer, I moved past clusters of flashing lights and passed myself under yellow crime scene tape. One of Austin's finest put up a hand to stop me, but Molly must have been watching for my arrival. She hurried over and ushered me through the small crowd of uniforms—steering me toward the dumpster.

With a warning look, she clicked her flashlight and shone it over the edge. My eyes reluctantly followed the beam. Inside, a dead girl lay like a discarded doll on a pile of trash. The knot in my empty stomach gave a queasy lurch as I realized I knew her. It was Jenny Summers, the beautiful, sometimes wayward daughter of Noble Summers. Even as my mind dutifully recorded details, the unfair immensity of her death wrapped chains around my heart and sunk it to the bottom of the world.

I'd known Jenny since way back when she was a cute little blonde teeny-bopper, flitting past UT football meeting rooms or hanging in the background—while her old man, by right of his generous donations to the program, ground out one of his infamous pep talks. Jenny had grown into a real dazzler, kind of wild the way rich girls can be. She was a slim, long-legged debutante who enchanted everyone with her happy-go-lucky smile and eyes the same electric blue as her father's.

The last time I'd seen Jenny had been in a nightclub off Congress. The missing person I'd been hired to find was sitting beside her, nuzzling her neck. The delighted, devilish grin lit Jenny's face when she saw me flashed through my mind with perfect clarity. I blinked back tears, and there she was, a sad, small human form hope had deserted, but death hadn't had a chance to claim—her face too white in the flashlight's glare, beauty otherwise intact.

Appraising me, Molly asked, "I saw Jenny hanging around the team often enough. I know you and Noble have history. You knew his daughter?"

"Yes, ma'am, well enough," I said with exaggerated courtesy, swallowing bile.

Even as college kids, Molly and I connected. Nothing romantic—we simply understood each other. That old bond radiated anger now as Molly frowned, reached down, and lifted the blue wool evening wrap covering Jenny's midsection. She directed her flash toward the dead girl's stomach. Sliced from pale unmoving breasts to pelvis, Jenny's intestines had been neatly arranged in a pile on the open cavity of her abdomen.

The smell hit me, and bile rose again in my throat. I coughed hoarsely, leaning back. "Jesus, Molly, give a guy a warning." I swallowed and closed my eyes, trying to concentrate. "How long has she been dead?"

Molly moved her flashlight up to features partially obscured by disheveled blonde hair. "Her facial muscles haven't stiffened. My guess is less than two hours. A Threadgill employee was taking out the trash, found her, and called 911. We've only been here about forty-five minutes." Molly rubbed the back of her neck. "It's Sunday morning, so no one else is about. It looks like the murderer dumped her in the bin, then surgically gutted her. There's no blood on the ground, but we'll know more after we move the body." Molly must have seen the winter in my grey eyes. She added in a gentler voice, "She would've died relatively quick."

I swallowed, looked aside from that brutal vivisection—focusing on Jenny's face while I struggled to regain composure. A light rain began to fall. Jenny's makeup distracted me as it tracked crooked lines down her empty features. I watched the last, false semblance to a living being wash away in that rain and the bleak November dawn. My few memories of Jenny alive melted into reality. This was just a corpse. Her animating soul had fled the violence and disappeared forever. I already had a strong suspicion where I fit into this evil scene, but I had to ask, "Molly, this is a police matter. Why have me come running?"

Molly replied carefully, "Old man Summers was pretty broken up when I called him about his daughter's death. He insisted I get you onto the crime scene asap and give you every cooperation possible."

Noble Summers was the owner of a local supermarket chain and an all-around good guy as far as the UT football program was concerned. I understood why he wanted me involved in his daughter's murder investigation. It wasn't anything I wanted to share, so I shrugged at the question in Molly's eyes. She raised an eyebrow but nodded to Sheryl Cook, the lead forensics investigator for Austin PD. It was time for CSI to take over.

Detective Molly O'Sullivan, freckle-skinned and red-headed, with hard lines and subtle curves, is more forcefully pretty than considered fashionable. She's a two-time State Judo Champ, and I've been to plenty of her tournaments. Compact and tightly wired, Molly fights with ruthless efficiency. She's not mean—she just doesn't believe in wasted motions. Frowning, Molly pivoted smartly and tossed back over her shoulder, "Harmon, let's take a ride out to Noble's house."

The rain found a path down the collar of my jacket, and a shiver ran up my spine. Noble Summers was much like the father I'd never had. Hell, what UT football alumni didn't owe something to Noble. Well, he'd just called in my markers, and that was okay by me. I was in—all the way in.

My anger grew—a slow, humming, electrical resonance itched and crawled under my skin. Taking a moment over Jenny's body, I prayed for her departed soul, then turned and followed Molly to her police cruiser. As I walked away from that empty shell of flesh, I made a promise to her memory. I'd give Jenny vengeance in kind. I knew her killer did not belong on this earth, and I vowed to correct that mistake.

Chapter 2 – A Distraught Father

G loomy autumn clouds ruled the morning sky, and a misty rain kept the cruiser's wipers on intermittent out to Noble's estate. There was no conversation—the mood in the cruiser as bleak as the day. Perched high above the Colorado River, the rustic lines of the new Pennybacker Bridge were rising into view as we turned left off Highway 360 and headed up the winding, steeply rising boulevard that led to Noble's home.

Home is perhaps too cozy a word. A palatial cluster of buildings, his sprawling estate took over where the road stopped and kept watch over the countryside from a dizzying height. Apart and alone, it stood proudly above the mansions of Austin's wealthiest. A set of wrought-iron gates with Longhorn symbols inlaid on matching panels barred entry. Molly had her window rolled down to punch the buzzer when the gates split and opened wide for us.

As we drove to the main house, sentinel yuccas guarded either side of the driveway, and a pair of dark wood, massively medieval-looking doors fronted the mansion's entrance. An honest-to-god butler, a tall, dark-haired, English-looking chap with a rock-steady demeanor, ushered us into the living room. The view out the south-facing bay windows made the high-walled, overstuffed room feel small. Miles of rolling hills swallowed the specks of lesser mortals' homes. We were suitably impressed.

Noble was perched on a white leather sectional, facing us. He stood politely, then bade us sit. Over six feet, all rawhide and gristle, the man radiated menace even under the best circumstances. Now, thunderclouds massed over silver puckered brows, and lightning lurked in ice-blue eyes. His dire gaze focused on me, but he demanded of Molly, "Detective O'Sullivan, what have you learned so far?"

Molly leaned forward. "Mr. Summers, I am sorry for your loss. I wish I had something more for you, but we came straight from the crime scene. I only know what I told you on the phone."

Noble kept his eyes on me. He'd known what Molly was going to say. "Harmon, you're my man on this. I know you won't stop until you find my daughter's killer." Noble added in a cold voice, "I can count on you." It was not so much question as harsh, hard statement.

Noble was a self-made man. He'd parlayed his father's oil rig profits into a chain of ultra-modern grocery stores. Last I heard, his N.E.S. Supermarkets were giving the major chains a run for their money in Texas. Used to making his own way and getting his way, the millions of dollars he put into his alma mater always had strings.

The particular debt I'd run up with him—when he threw the first few jobs my way, way back when I was scrambling to find people who'd pay an ex-soldier with a brand-new license to do detective work—also had strings. Trouble was, I had no right to say no to this proud, old man and every reason to say yes, in spite or perhaps because of what I intended to do about the evil I'd sensed in that parking lot.

I nodded grimly. "Yeah, I'm your man."

Noble's shoulders sagged. His anger had been a false front, desperately needing to hear that I would help. When a parent loses their only child, the foundation of their life collapses under them. I could feel Noble suffering like one already damned. He ground out, "Good." Then surprised me by adding, "Thank you." under his breath.

Molly asked, "Mr. Summers, is there anything you can tell us that might help find your daughter's murderer?"

Noble shook his head sadly, "Jenny didn't keep in close contact. I don't know what she's been up to." He paused before reluctantly adding, "Just what I hear around town." He bowed his head, then looked back up and with more strength in his voice, said, "She visited maybe once a month. I bought her a penthouse in those newfangled Towers of Town Lake Condos on the river downtown. I can give you the address." He became lost in faraway thoughts, then gave a small start. "I'll call the manager to let you into her place."

Molly nodded, "We'll need to check her bank account and credit cards for unusual money flows, and we'll check any other records we can find. Did she have a car phone?"

Noble said, "My office took care of her expenses." He moved to a nearby table, wrote on a pad, tore the page off, and handed it to Molly. "This is my personal secretary's name and number and Jenny's home and mobile numbers."

Molly thanked him. "Mr. Summers, do you have any recent photos of Jennifer you could let us borrow?"

"I do." Noble disappeared into the rear of his home. He returned with a handful of 5x7s showing differing poses from the same session. Jenny wore a simple silk strap top and an expensive pair of buckskin-colored jeans. High-heeled pumps enhanced her long legs. Her sunny personality graced every photo.

Noble told us, "These are from a shoot I set up when she got it in her head she wanted to be a fashion model. By the time the photos were ready, she was off on another tangent. She couldn't be bothered, so I had my secretary pick them up." He kept ahold of one shot, his gaze locked onto her face. A tear fell on the page, staining Jenny's sweet smile. "I don't believe she ever even saw 'em." Noble turned back to me. "Harmon, you're a good boy. You've always done what's right. I heard how you helped that poor banker."

What I did to the maniac who murdered Robert Morrow's son, then two more people in rapid succession, was just as illegal as what I intended for Jenny's murderer. I'd figured that was why the old man corralled me so quickly, but I ll winced mentally. From the corner of my eye, I could see Molly's quizzical look and a hint of suspicion in her emerald eyes. I thought we might just have more conversation on the way back than we'd had on the way out.

Noble climbed to his feet, head lowered, sunk in his own grief. He hadn't even realized what he'd said. I stepped across the intervening space and hugged him, willing comfort into my embrace. Noble tensed for a moment, then sagged against me, pressing a muffled sob into my shoulder. When the old man raised his eyes to mine, his features were etched like battered iron, and his anger filled the space between us. "Harmon, she's gone. She was my miracle. Now my little girl's gone. The one who took her from me doesn't deserve to be on this Earth."

His words echoed my earlier thoughts, and silent agreement passed between us. Noble reached into his jeans pocket and pushed a wad of bills into my hand before he stepped back. "This will get you started. You let me know what else you need." Noble's ice blue eyes stayed locked on mine. "Anything. Anything at all I can do, I will do." I understood his offer was for more than just money. I nodded, never breaking eye contact. Molly coughed. Yeah, we were going to have things to talk about.

Noble escorted us back to the front door, then grasped my arm like he was holding onto his life. "Harmon, you've got my number." Opening the door, he turned to Molly and, with a hint of the power he'd shown when we first walked in, said, "Detective O'Sullivan, I've been in touch with the mayor. You have some help coming too."

We headed down the steps, and when I looked back, Noble Summers still stood there, the shattered shadow of a larger-than-life man. I already missed the old Noble and wondered if I would ever see that once indomitable giant again.

Chapter 3 – Where There's Smoke

Showers ended, clouds scattered, and the temperature continued to rise. Mother Nature took a lousy morning and swept it into a mild Texas afternoon. The drive back hadn't been fun. Sidestepping Molly's questions kept me busy until she decided she'd had enough of me. From Highway 183 on, I was treated to cold silence. We'd already planned on looking for clues in Jenny's condo at 4 pm, so Molly dropped me off in the lunch-crowded Threadgill's parking lot and drove off, her face sour and distant.

When I finally got out of the Rangers and back to Austin, I'd hired a taxi to carry me from Mueller Airport to the Miracle Mile—a row of car dealers fronting the east side of I-35, just south of Ben White Boulevard. I drove out of the second dealership in a shivery cool, silver 1979 BMW 320i convertible. It had 145,000 miles on the odometer, but that's nothing for a BMW. Four years, thirty-seven-some-odd-thousand miles, and regular oil changes later, it still ran like a top. I stowed the BMW's roof and gave a nod to the officer parked near the tape-festooned dumpster.

A dark shadow seemed to follow me out of the lot, but I let the cool midday breeze slide past the throbbing in my temples. Heading south on Lamar, I tried to ignore the hammering of mad, bad thoughts and focus on the sunny Sunday afternoon. Traffic was light, the eclectic businesses crowding both sides of the gently winding road being mostly closed. Soon enough, I was traveling through a short stack of scattered skyscrapers.

Passing through and out of downtown, I crossed over the placidly rolling Colorado River on the old Lamar Boulevard Bridge. A concrete span constructed during a WWII iron shortage, the bridge was a stately transit with more innate character than most of its steel sisters—except the Pennybacker. Swinging east on Riverside, I absently checked out the Austinites taking advantage of the bearable afternoon sun to frequent the still green, open vistas lining Auditorium Shores.

Familiar sights and smells, the wind whipping my hair, the road itself—these were tonics typically helped center my thoughts. I needed to get a handle on my next move, but the memory of Jenny's ruined makeup running down her face kept blindsiding rational thought. I still had a couple of hours before I needed to meet Molly at Jenny's condo. Taking a right on South Congress, I headed for a hole-in-the-wall bar I knew stocked quality whiskeys.

My tires crunched on gravel as I pulled into a mostly empty lot next to the bar. There were only two vehicles: a faded green Buick sedan eclipsed by a 1952 Hudson Hornet boasting a paint job the same shade as bluebonnets and stylized red flames splashed across fenders and hood. I stopped on my way into the bar to peer in the cool classic's window and saw that it even had the original blue interior. Whistling an appreciative note, I walked around the corner, pushed open the door, and stepped into the dim interior.

As my eyes adjusted, I could see the barkeep at his station and a single customer sitting at a far corner table—a massive man with Native American features. I nodded, and he inclined his head slightly. Taking a stool at the bar, I checked the bourbons on a chalk menu and ordered a Maker's Mark on the rocks. The spare, grizzle-haired bartender poured my drink, then disappeared into the back, where I could hear him moving boxes.

I savored my first sip and took a deep, calming breath. Before I could take a second, the sense of a presence behind me disturbed my tentative peace. Glancing over my left shoulder, I saw—nothing. To my right, the giant still sat propped against the wall. Okay, maybe I was imagining things, but I couldn't shake the sense of impending danger. It was as though I sat in a sniper's crosshairs. Feeling stupidly paranoid, I downed my drink in one swallow and hunched over the empty glass.

Like a shotgun blast, a sudden lancing pain nearly took my head off!

My brain was pounded raw in an instant. Still dimly aware, still sitting at the bar, I raised one trembling hand to my face, expecting to touch—what? Maybe blood pouring from burst vessels. It hurt that much. The outside world dwindled to a faraway thought, and I heard laughter in the darkness inside my head—nasty, utterly vicious laughter.

Time slowed to a stop. I stood at my own side, looking at myself, slumped over, head on my arms. A thought intruded on my pain, *There shouldn't be laughter.* That sickly, bubbling amusement abruptly rose to a manic pitch. Agony overwhelmed, and I fell into it, sinking under the weight of a torment somehow tied to that dark, demented mirth.

A small, clear conscious thought saw light and reached for it. The pain ceased as abruptly as it had begun and I sensed a warm reassurance perched on my right shoulder. I realized it was a hand and ran my reassembling thoughts over the words I'd heard. Their meaning became clear second time around: "Can I buy you another drink?"

I turned, and a red plaid shirt filled my returning vision. I looked up and up into the craggy face of the man who'd been sitting in the corner. My first inane thought was, "That's one big Indian."

"Sure," I mumbled, not capable of saying more.

The large man took a seat on the stool next to me. It didn't help; I still had to tilt my head way back to look him in the eyes. He stuck out a bear-sized right hand, and his heavy voice rumbled in his chest like an echo of thunder. "My name is Smoke on Distant Mountain, but everyone calls me Smoke."

I let his enormous paw engulf mine and said, "Waite," in a voice that cracked. I tried again, "My name is Harmon Waite." We shook hands.

I saw the big Indian glance over my shoulder, and from the corner of my eye, caught movement in the mirror behind the bar. I swung around to look and could have sworn a shadow passed out through sunlight filtering in from the stained-glass sign in the bar's front window. I blinked; my eyes must be playing tricks on me. When I turned back to Smoke, I noticed a frown and started to say something. Then his eyes returned to mine, and his frown transformed into a peaceful smile so gentle it felt like a gift.

The bartender came back to check on us, and Smoke rumbled, "Two Maker on the rocks, please." I shook off the notion—but couldn't shake an eerie sensation that this big man had just been or would become important in my life. I have premonitions every so often. I always pay attention to them. Lifting my glass, I toasted Smoke and took a tentative sip. The whiskey burned going down. It was a solid, well-remembered fire—and just like that, the world was an ordinary place again.

Smoke asked, "Are you all right?" I studied him with momentary suspicion. "For a moment, you looked like you were about to fall off your bar stool. I was a medic in the war, and it looked like you were having some kind of seizure. I came over to see if you needed help. By the time I got here, you'd started pulling yourself together. I was not mistaken about your distress?" He queried me again, concern tinging his voice, "You are all right?"

I shook my head. "Yeah, I'm fine now. I'm not sure what happened. Maybe I got hit by a train." I looked around for an elusive set of train tracks.

Smoke gave a short bark of laughter. "Okay, Mr. Harmon Waite."

I changed the subject. "So, Smoke is an interesting name, but Smoke on Distant Mountain? That's a mouthful."

Smoke took the comment as a question, and a slight gleam sparked at the back of his golden eyes. No, not gold, brown. I shook my head—for a moment, I could've sworn he had gold eyes. Smoke declared in an oddly formal tone, "My father was a Cherokee shaman, a medicine man. I barely knew him. My mother died when I was young, so grandmother raised me. She was very traditional. Many of my people adopted white man names, but she always used my Cherokee name. I have lived with it for a long time."

My wits were still addled, but I thought the story a bit strange. I told him I was sorry about his parents. Smoke shrugged, shoulders like shifting mountains. "I do not know what kept my father away. He was gone for good while I was still a boy. My grandmother rarely spoke of him, but she told me the name my father had given me was important to him."

I was faintly embarrassed for inadvertently making Smoke share personal details of his life with a stranger. He grinned at my expression. "Harmon Waite, you should not feel bad. I hardly knew my father and mother, but the last years of my grandmother's life, what was left of her world, was built around raising me. I did not suffer more than others of my tribe."

I knew there must be much more to his story, but I was too close to prying. Looking him up and down, I judged, "Well, your dad must have been a large man, anyway."

Smoke replied somberly, "Yes, he was a very big man."

I couldn't help myself; I laughed. It felt so good I laughed again. "Smoke, let me buy you a drink this time."

"OK, Harmon Waite," Smoke replied with another spreading, sunlit smile.

We talked while we worked on the next round. Communication was easy, as if we'd known each other for years. When I remembered to check my watch, I jumped to my feet and said, "Smoke, I've got to run; I'm late for a date." I threw some bills on the bar and extracted a plain black and white business card from my wallet. "You don't know how much you've helped me today. If you want to give me a call sometime, I'd enjoy finding a suitable place and continuing this conversation."

"Yes," Smoke rumbled, "Fishing is an excellent way to get to know a friend."

I paused on my way out the door. Friend? That sounded right. I wasn't a fisherman, but the thought of an afternoon spent tossing baited lines into one of the nearby lakes with the big man was a peaceful one. "Fishing works for me. See you soon, then."

"Yes, I expect you will," Smoke replied. He sounded damned enigmatic when he said that. Perhaps it was the alcohol. It had already been a long day, but I was ready for the next task. I'd find a clue at Jenny Summers' place to put me on the track of her killer. I had to. I didn't have any other leads.

Chapter 4 – One Small Clue

On the way to Jenny's condo, I reflected on the severe brain whupping I'd endured in that bar. I decided it was too intense for a migraine or even a heart attack. Although I'm no doctor, I couldn't really imagine a likely physical cause. Stranger still was the fact that on the heels of my next drink, everything went right back to normal.

I did a quick inventory. Yup, no physical aftereffects. Thank God for that. I considered the one thing I did know. Puzzling, even impossible as it may be, I could still hear an echo of that evil laughter in the wind whipping around my windshield. The laughter might not make a lick of sense, but it felt real. I wasn't willing to discount it simply because I didn't understand. The more I pondered, the more likely I figured it and the pain I'd experienced must be bound up together.

Wincing inwardly at its fanciful direction, I pursued the strange thread as I turned east onto 1st Street and headed downtown. The pain had been overwhelming. As soon as that white light showed up, though—at that exact moment—both the torment and the obnoxious laughter ceased. Had that been my doing? No, it had been Smoke's hand on my shoulder derailed the train running over my brain.

I shook my head. *How the Horatio?*

The world was larger than my philosophies. I'd experienced enough strange events during my Ranger days to fill a book. Even a few of my investigations over the years, like the Morrow case, had descended into the bizarre. Some questions have no good answers, at least none any rational view of this world supports.

I was deep in troubled thought when a shadow touched my rearview mirror. It could have been from one of the surrounding buildings. Yeah, could have. A sudden memory of darkness that moved toward the light and a sense of renewed menace belied that idea. I focused on the road, watching for a safe place to pull over just in case.

It may have been silly. Maybe not. I drove carefully but reached Jenny's place without seeing any other lurking shades. More importantly, without a recurrence of what I was starting to think of as a psychic attack. My next stop would have to be the church. I needed a convo with God before this day got any stranger.

When the doorman opened the fancy wood and glass doors to the Towers of Town Lake Condos for me, Molly was already in the lobby, looking impatient as she conversed in low tones with a polite-looking fellow I took to be the manager. They both turned, and Molly frowned. She laid a forefinger on her watch. "Yeah, my bad," I muttered absently, thinking about something I'd noticed.

Molly introduced the thin, dapper man as Mr. Preston, the Towers manager. We shook hands, and Mr. Preston took the lead saying, "Follow me, please."

Molly frowned again as I asked them to give me a moment. A small thrill of anticipation fluttered in my chest. Even though he maintained his professional air, I could tell the doorman had something to say when I passed him. He was my height but broader built, boasting a fit vitality and a still-dark tan told me he was playing outdoors when he wasn't working indoors.

I strode over and stuck out my hand, "Afternoon, my name's Harmon Waite."

He took my hand automatically. "Jimmy Cowart." Although surprised, he considered his manager, then said more formally, "James Cowart."

I smiled and asked, "Jimmy, you knew Jenny Summers?"

"Um," he responded, looking to his boss.

Mr. Preston waved a hand and said, "James, this is Detective O'Sullivan and her partner, Harmon Waite. They're looking into Jenny Summers' murder. Please tell them anything you think might help."

Jimmy was itching to tell us, but he started tentatively. "Well, you see, I was on duty yesterday when Miss Summers came through the lobby. It was dinner time, but she was dressed for the evening." He fumbled his next words, "Um, I'm not trying to say anything, but she wasn't really outfitted for a meal. She wore a red skirt with sequins and a big diamond necklace."

He swallowed an emotion and continued, "Anyway, I held the door open for her. She got into a fancy car with this big guy." Sadness weighed the boyish lines of his face. "I got off work pretty soon after that. You'll have to check with the night doorman to be sure, but I don't guess anyone here saw her again."

Molly slid past me as I opened my mouth with a follow-up question, "James, thank you. What can you tell me about the man?"

"Oh, I just got a glimpse of him. I wasn't trying to stare or anything."

"No problem, James," Molly said soothingly. "Do you remember the color of his hair?"

"It was dark, so I'm not sure of the color, but it was cut short, like a businessman's. That's the impression I got of him: that he was a businessman. Older than Jenny, too; maybe even in his forties. Jenny jumped right in the car with him, though, and they took off real quick."

"What kind of car exactly?"

Jimmy didn't have to think twice. "A Mercedes, I remember the symbol. It was a big sedan, and it looked brand new." He added as an afterthought, "It was charcoal colored."

I jumped back into the questioning. "Jimmy, how do you know he was a big guy?"

Jimmy brightened. "Because he took up the entire driver's side. The outside lights were on by then, and they're really bright, but I could only see small patches of light behind him." He added apologetically, "He was mostly in shadow."

Molly said, "So, you didn't see his face?"

"Not any features I remember, ma'am, just an impression that he was older," Jimmy replied politely.

Molly checked with me. I shrugged, so she turned back to the doorman. "Jimmy, can you please stick around. I'll be right back, and I may have a few more questions for you."

Jimmy replied easily, "No problem, ma'am. My shift isn't over for another hour."

Molly thanked him, and we headed to the elevator with Mr. Preston. He talked about Jenny on our ride up—idle gossip, nothing that bore on her murder. Although he referenced Noble, he seemed not to have met him. When we arrived at the apartment, Mr. Preston opened the door with a master key and deferentially excused himself.

I took the front of the condo, and Molly headed back to Jenny's bedroom. After a careful search, we compared notes. Everything looked normal—a bit messy, hardly any food in the fridge, etc. There were no messages, computer to check, address book, or even a calendar on the wall. I did notice one thing, a matchbook from The Continental Club sitting on the coffee table. It was missing a few matches.

The Continental is an iconic nightclub on South Congress, hot again after a complete facelift earlier this year. What made the find curious—it was the same club where Jenny had flashed me that impish grin during my missing person's search. Maybe The Continental was a regular hangout for her. It was a thread barely big enough to grasp. I didn't bother mentioning it to Molly but decided dropping by the club later wouldn't hurt.

On the way out, Molly snorted in disgust. "They found a bunch of fake diamonds in the dumpster, obviously from the necklace Jimmy saw on her. No other evidence. In particular, no saliva, semen, or skin under her nails. It's damned strange—like she didn't fight back." As we arrived at the elevator, she gestured back toward Jenny's apartment. "Sheryl and her crew will be here shortly. I hope they find more than we did."

We rode down in silence, but as the doors opened, Molly volunteered, "I'm going to try to pry more details out of Jimmy, and I'll have my team follow up on the man our victim went out with last night. They'll make a run at finding the vehicle. We'll also check popular nightclubs and restaurants for anyone who might have seen Jenny with an older man. Molly paused, then prompted, "Pretty thin, huh. Harmon, any thoughts?"

I hedged, "Nothing worth noting. I'm going to scout around the downtown clubs myself." I could tell Molly was still miffed from earlier, but she nodded goodbye before she stopped to chat with Jimmy.

I walked out into an afternoon already dwindling into night. I was headed for the Cathedral of St. Mary off Brazos—a part of Austin's heart and history—and my personal refuge. It was also a place that held my only other hope for a lead—the matchbook idea being so thin I could barely breathe on it without expecting it to go up in smoke.

Chapter 5 - The Cathedral of Saint Mary

I'm not claiming the Catholic church has it right, but the weight of their traditions is always a comfort, never a drag on my spirit. When I walk into a church, God is not an abstract concept—He's real.

As soon as I stepped inside the Cathedral of Saint Mary, I felt His presence—the stately gravity of that venerable old building supporting the sense of something greater than my small self. Built back in the 1870s, about the time Texas was rejoining the union after the devastations of the Civil War, its stone spires and tall stained-glass windows are a remnant of the frontier nestled in the heart of our modern city. I knelt in a pew toward the front where I could contemplate the stained-glass Mary and the dark blue starry sky of the chancel dome—her glory and the inspiration of a larger Universe helping overshadow the painful sight of the hanging Christ.

I said two prayers, one to Jesus and one to Mary, then sat down on the bench, closed my eyes, and leaned into my mind to have a heart-to-heart with God. It wasn't a real conversation. God doesn't answer me with words. But when I revisited the crime scene in my head, I felt the instant conviction that I was indeed up against something inherently evil. This was not a crime of human passion like a lover spurned or a man obsessed.

I was dealing with a cold, deadly force that inflicted pain for the joy of it and killed to satiate its own sick lusts.

I approached the dumpster again and, looking around carefully, noted the lack of clues. Peering in, I saw Jenny's body. Every detail of her death was apparent. I saw her still-intact beauty. The lack of bruises on arms and legs. Her azure blue evening wrap, which I expected she'd picked out to compliment her eyes, covering the awful mutilation. Underneath, her red sequined skirt was split by a single clean stroke. Those same neat slices parted the flesh of her abdomen, and her intestines, expertly removed, were piled on her open stomach.

My mind turned of its own accord to the bar attack. I didn't quite know what He was saying, but I realized that Jenny's death was somehow tied to the shadow of menace I'd experienced that afternoon. It made little sense, but when God speaks, it's best to listen.

I replayed that instant when the shadow flowed through stained glass—watching it disappear by slow degrees. Then I went a bit further back in time and felt the relief pouring into me when Smoke on Distant Mountain laid his hand on my shoulder. It was his light that disrupted the psychic attack. God nudged, and I understood that gentle giant hadn't been sitting in that bar by accident.

My thoughts drifted, letting the day's minutiae dance their random patterns before my awareness. I was stalking the elusive facts hide behind the apparent, and what I found disturbed me. Humans are not the apex predators they think they are. Evil is an absolute and active presence in this world. I've seen it manifest before and knew I was seeing it again.

There are only two things anyone can do when evil comes calling—run or fight. For me, only one response has ever worked. I have to fight. Corruption is a potent enemy, but faith is the shortest distance between two points. It is the perfect response. I had faith I would find Jenny's killer and faith I would banish that evil presence from the world.

God smiled. I grinned back.

My eyes drifted open, and I meditated on Christ on the Cross while my connection with the Almighty faded. I had confirmed a couple of things. One, what I was facing wasn't any ordinary murderer. Two, I wanted to see Smoke again. I climbed out of the pew, genuflected, and on my way out, admired, as I always did, the gold, the stained glass, and the rich wood beams—all combining to resurrect that sense of the old world in the new. As I crossed the cathedral's threshold, I dabbed my forefingers in the marbled bowl of holy water and made the sign of the cross.

Chapter 6 - Down the Rabbit Hole

While I was in the church, darkness had fallen—the Texas night turning a pleasant afternoon into autumn again. It was brisk, but the night sky was clear of clouds and full of stars. I needed to get home, grab a bite, change clothes, and head to The Continental Club. My visit with God put some things in perspective but hadn't yielded new clues, so that was my last immediate hope for a way forward.

Once home, I hopped in and out of the shower, wolfed down a bowl of leftover stew, then dressed in jeans, comfortable cowboy boots, and a black cotton shirt. To be safe, I fastened my knife to my leg and strapped the rig holstering my Colt .45 over my shoulders. Then, I threw on my bomber jacket and headed back out.

A waning moon enlivened the crystal-clear night, and I left the BMW's top down while I drove, enjoying the sting of cold air. Too soon, I was on South Congress again. I glanced at the stained glass in the window as I passed that same hole-in-the-wall bar and noticed the Hudson Hornet still in the parking lot.

The Continental Club was a long block further on, and I pulled into an uncrowded lot nearby. There weren't many people on the street and even fewer in the club. What there were differed from the 6th Street crowd—less black clothing, more ponytails. I glanced around the seedy interior. At one of the few occupied tables, a giant sat sipping a bottle of beer. Slipping between the tables, not waiting for an invite, I took a seat. "Smoke, good to see you again. What the heck are you doing here?"

His eyes twinkled in the dark. "Hello again, Harmon Waite. I am having a drink. Join me?"

"Since I'm already here, believe I will." I leaned back in my chair and eyed the big man quizzically. "Wanna hear something interesting?" He raised an eyebrow. "I had a talk with God earlier. He said you being in that bar today was no coincidence. I tend to agree with Him."

Smoke smiled. "I never disagree with God."

"So, here you are again. What's up?" I asked more deliberately.

Smoke responded seriously, a trait I was getting used to. "You might call it a premonition. I know I need to be here now, just as I knew I needed to be in that bar earlier."

"Why?"

"Harmon Waite, I could not have answered that until I met you. Now, I will say I believe there is a light the universe doesn't want extinguished."

I wondered how he could be talking about me and said, "You know that sounds like bullshit, don't you?"

Smoke did not smile this time. "Yes, Harmon Waite, it does."

"OK, I'm willing to bite on whatever you're selling—if you can tell me how you stopped the pain from that damned attack earlier. And yeah, I'm sure it was an attack. That same Guy told me so."

Smoke considered what he wanted to do, spar with me or answer directly. He compromised by doing both. "My father was full of magic. I inherited some of it."

I was considering the reasons Smoke would call a medicine man magical when a terrified scream pierced the club's atmosphere. It came from the street. Smoke and I exchanged glances, then I pushed my chair back and slid between the tables. Behind me, I heard Smoke shoving tables out of his way as he followed. We hit the door shoulder to shoulder. The screaming continued, rising in pitch—issuing from a narrow alley next to the club.

We pounded into the alley at a dead run, starlight keeping us from bouncing off brick walls. A dark figure ahead towered over a sprawled form. The silver flash of a blade was followed by a chopping thud, and that same horrible scream echoed the alley's length. I pulled my pistol from its shoulder holster. Unable to aim at center mass for fear of hitting his victim, I fired three quick rounds at the assailant's head, then launched myself.

I noticed a distorted glimmer in the air behind them precisely as her attacker turned, leapt through, and disappeared. Smoke yelled, "Wait!" I wasn't sure if he was calling my name or telling me to stop.

A single headlong step more, and I hurtled into that same shimmering patch of night. Falling into emptiness, I tumbled down a steep slope that should not, could not have been there, hit bottom, lost my grip, and heard my pistol clatter away. Rolling, I came to my feet in absolute darkness. There was no light, no sound. It was as though I'd fallen into the earth itself.

A familiar ugly laugh rolled over me, and a voice like grinding glass taunted, "Looking for me, bright boy?" I dove hard to my left and heard metal strike ground, then a grunt of frustration. I came out of the roll onto my feet, hesitating. I shouldn't move without knowing what was around me, but I could hear that blade. It was swinging in deadly arcs I couldn't see. A nasty chuckling accompanied the swishing sound.

"Give me some freakin' light!" It was half prayer, half explicative, but a silvery light sprang up as if at my command. It lit a weird grey landscape, more shadow than substance. A huge, misshapen figure paused in that pale glow, then resumed swinging a wicked-looking straight razor. Manlike, it towered over me, features swathed in a darkness that seemed to absorb the wan light. What I could see was distorted, as though viewed through warped glass. Not knowing exactly what I faced, I was sure it was no ordinary man. I was also damned positive I was no longer in my own world.

I remembered what I'd seen on the alley floor before I fell down the rabbit hole. It had been a young girl, very much like Jenny, eyes open wide in frantic horror and pain. A wave of calming anger washed over me. I didn't look around. I wasn't worried about where we were. This was the same monster I'd promised Jenny I'd stop. He was standing right in front of me.

I reached down and slid my knife from its ankle sheath. I've carried it since my army days, and I offered a prayer of thanks for that good, old habit. Its wicked seven-inch blade over-matched the murderer's straight razor. I felt the confidence of my Ranger training, reinforcing my absolute certainty that this monstrous entity needed to be destroyed.

The creature continued making broad, arcing slashes that flashed fitfully in the dimness. Time slowed, and the streaking gleams of the straight razor became a wavering dance. I closed into range, leaned away from a gleeful slash, and effortlessly stepped into his swing's backside. The murderer's momentum exposed the bulk of his shoulder, and I drove my knife deep into unnaturally resistant flesh. Though it parted for my sharp steel, only wispy smoke escaped. There was no blood.

The fiend bellowed, sounding angrier than hurt, and his other arm snaked out of his shadowy mass, grabbing me by the neck. Whipping my blade out, I stabbed into the flesh of that enormous forearm—again to little effect. He shook me as a terrier shakes a rat, then tossed me aside contemptuously. I tucked and rolled, swallowed to make sure I still could, then launched myself low, trying to topple his bulk and get him to the ground where I might do some damage.

It was like hitting oak tree stumps. My left shoulder went numb as I fell back, then rolled to avoid the massive foot stomping down to crush my skull. Adrenaline bounced me up and backed me away. It felt like I'd broken my collarbone, and it hurt to swallow, but I still held my knife defensively in my right hand.

Wobbling on unsteady feet, the slow-motion sense of time tiptoeing past deserted me as the pain in my shoulder throbbed, synced to the hammering of my heart. At that moment, clear as only memory can be, Jenny's face, her electric eyes alive with mischief, danced across my clouded vision. My aches disappeared—the calm anger I'd felt gave way to a storm of white-hot rage didn't clear my senses but kept me standing.

Inhuman laughter bubbled deep within the brute's chest. "What the hell are you?" I demanded.

"What the hell are you?" the grating voice mimicked.

As the fiend raised his razor and I lunged, my knife held high for a killing stroke, I glimpsed a human form rising behind the monster and saw a silver flash. Six inches of steel abruptly protruded from the murderer's massive rib cage, and he threw up his arms, roaring with pain even as my knife plunged down—driving to the hilt in his chest. It continued sinking into a physical body suddenly less than flesh. Light exploded from my fist inside that dark mass, and the seemingly supernatural creature shattered into smoking mists.

I was left staring at a woman with long silver hair and eyes that shone like indigo sapphires in the dim light. She stood, sword in hand, gazing back at me with something akin to my own awe in her fierce blue eyes. "Did we kill it?" I wondered out loud.

"No," she replied steadily enough but with a trace of sorrow, "Jack is not so easily destroyed here in Purgatory, but we hurt him. He has likely returned to Hell to lick his wounds and work himself into a fury over us."

That was a lot to take in—but my savior distracted most of my attention. Except for the lack of pointed ears, she could have been a warrior elf queen out of *The Lord of the Rings*. She had angular features in a cupid face made even more exotic by heart-shaped lips. Her eyes burned with those cold, cerulean flames and her limbs were long, lean, and graceful. Before I could say anything, she turned toward a nearby slope in the land. Sitting at its summit, I could see a shimmering disturbance, the gate between worlds I had fallen through. She spoke a word that thrummed with energy, and the doorway faded.

"Wasn't that our way home?" I asked, still preoccupied with her almost angelic beauty but a bit concerned nonetheless.

She gifted me with a decidedly impish smile. "I imagine the police will be on the other side of that particular portal by now. A suspect I don't want to be. How about you?" Without waiting for my bemused response, she added, "There's more than one way out of this place."

While I struggled to absorb everything that had happened, I found my pistol and holstered my weapons. My rescuer neatly slid her sword into a scabbard slung across her back and set off with long, confident strides across the nearly featureless landscape. I hurried to catch up, wondering which of the thousand questions crowding my brain I could safely ask first.

Chapter 7 – The Ripper

The formless terrain morphed from grassy-soft to a sandier slog. If this was Purgatory, it was as empty as 6th Street on a Sunday morning. I processed the weirdness while we walked. Though rabbit-hole strange, I didn't feel like moaning about it. I'd had encounters with inexplicable phenomena in my past. Rather than doubt, my experiences had taught me it could be lifesaving to focus on what my eyes showed me—instead of what my brain wanted to believe.

I remembered one odd thing and decided to try an experiment. "More light!" I commanded. When the world around me brightened perceptibly, I sucked in a breath and let it out as a chuckle. My companion glanced back, a pretty frown on her elfin features. "What?" I asked, shrugging, then winced as my shoulder reminded me it was on the heavily bruised side of not broken.

"Your power is showing." She must have seen the confusion on my face because she added, "When you exert power, you reveal your true nature. Those inhabitants of Purgatory who tend to notice any display of the kind of power you have might then decide to test you. In fact, most would delight in doing so."

I looked around—everything was bland to the nth degree. Since my fight, I hadn't seen or heard a single sign of a living presence. "Purgatory looks pretty empty to me."

"Not empty," she replied. "Large. Very, very large."

Despite the questions banging around in my head, politeness came first. "My name is Harmon Waite. What's yours?"

My savior glanced back again, "I am Eirian." She pronounced it Eye-Ree-Anne with a musical lilt. I repeated her name, my Texas accent stretching the brogue trill. Eirian's lips quirked, "You have questions, Mr. Waite. Please ask. I will tell you what I can."

I immediately said, "You were following me?"

"No," she replied, "I was following Jack. You just got in the way."

"Jack? That's the name of the creature we fought, the one that blew itself to pieces but is not really dead?"

"Correct. Jack is one of the Grigori, a group of accursed devils. I've been on his trail since the last time he was here in Austin, murdering young women under a different guise. That was back in 1886. I thought I'd ended him for good back then, but like us, devils can be hard to properly kill. Although my blessed blade thrust cleanly through his vile heart, and we buried the body, it was only a couple of years before he regained the power to travel to Earth again. He showed up in London in 1888, calling himself Jack and slicing up prostitutes."

I nearly stumbled, "Do you mean Jack, as in Jack the Ripper?"

"Yes."

Worlds were opening before my eyes. I took refuge in levity. "You don't look a day over twenty-nine."

Eirian laughed. It was a trinkling delight. "I am much older than that. We are all long-lived, Harmon Waite."

"We?"

She stopped and turned back to me, her lovely eyebrows rising. "You do not know?"

"Know what? I know none of this makes sense. I'm not blind or dumb, so I also know what we fought was no kind of man." I sobered. "And

I know I'm one lucky sob you came along when you did. Thank you, Eirian. You saved my life back there."

She gave me an appraising look. "How old are you, Mr. Waite?"

"Thirty-one."

"Only a baby, then. You have much to learn." She softened her pronouncement with a gentle grin. It was the damnedest thing; when she smiled, I felt blessed. I wondered what it would take to get her to laugh again.

Eirian changed the subject abruptly, "We are in what some call Purgatory. Jack, who was named The Ripper by old London for good reason, can't be killed here because he is strong this close to Hell and can move easily between physical and etheric bodies. Flesh binds him more strongly on the mortal plane, so we can hurt him, but it takes a blade blessed like my Dyrnwyn."

She reached back, patted her sword's hilt, was silent for a moment, then started walking again. I heard her mutter, "I should have burned Jack's body instead of burying it." I was considering that the world was, once again, proving itself no ordinary place when Eirian halted abruptly. "Here we are."

I wondered how she figured out she needed to stop here versus ten feet further along or ten feet back. I waited. She closed her eyes as though offering a prayer, and it took me a moment to catch the phosphorescence as it dusted the still air. Spreading out, it appeared more like a door with each passing instant. Before long, a thick, irregular curtain of light hung before us, dim but definite.

Eirian checked to ensure I was paying attention, then bent low and stepped through that fragile-looking, world-spanning portal. I followed close upon her heels as she disappeared from view, careful not to touch the edges. Passing through, I crossed back into the cool of the Texas night. The sights and smells of my world rushed in, and I realized how genuinely empty Purgatory had been.

We were in the parking lot of that same hole-in-the-wall bar. As if he'd been waiting for us, Smoke leaned stoically against the driver's door of the Hudson Hornet. I wasn't the least bit surprised by his presence but kicked myself for not guessing the Hornet belonged to him.

Introductions were in order, so I said, "Eirian, this is Smoke. He saved my bacon earlier this afternoon."

I turned to Smoke. "Smoke, this is Eirian. A few minutes ago, she saved my life"—adding under my breath—"on what is turning into one champion of a strange day." A sweep of my arm took in both my companions and the bar. "Can I please thank you by buying you both a drink?"

Eirian acquiesced by reaching back to touch the hilt of her slung sword—which appeared to simply disappear. I nodded toward the now invisible blade. "Neat trick that." She looked at me without comment. Smoke grunted and, levering his massive form away from his cool car, led the way into the bar.

Chapter 8 – The Larger Arc

We sat at the same corner table Smoke had occupied earlier. The bar was still empty, and the same grizzled bartender was wiping the counter. I wondered if he was the owner and, if so, how he stayed in business. He seemed a likely optimist as he had help tonight from a pretty waitress. Her brunette hair was tied in a ponytail, and she had a well-rounded figure for a youngster. She looked delighted to see us or, more likely, any potentially tipping customer. It wasn't much of a stretch to figure she was a UT student since she left a stack of textbooks to bounce over and take our order.

We decided on two Makers and a Chardonnay. When the drinks arrived, I handed the wine to Eirian and silently toasted them both. Smoke raised his glass, but Eirian wasn't paying attention. She was busy looking Smoke up and down, a rather lengthy process. Smoke turned to regard her in return. "You are demi-divine?" she finally asked.

After a glance at me, Smoke replied, "Through my father, a medicine man."

"How many generations removed?"

"Only one."

She leaned back. "I am not surprised. I could see your light from the other side. You made the choice of exits easy."

I sighed. "Eirian, whenever you open your mouth, my brain sprouts another dozen questions. Before we go there, and I do hope you're willing to indulge me, will you please catch Smoke up on what happened in Purgatory with that creature and what you told me? I'm sure it'll help me get things straight in my head."

She nodded, and I sipped my whiskey while Eirian recited the tale of our short fight with, and her longer hunt of Jack the Ripper. When she mentioned her previous visit to Austin, I asked, "What year was that again?"

She replied, "The first time I tracked down that murdering devil was in February 1886. He'd already killed eight women here in Austin. I ran my sword through him while he was busy murdering a ninth. An Austin sheriff, John Bracken, entered the house where we were and put a bullet in his spine. Jack dropped dead, and we buried his body in consecrated ground. I thought I was rid of that particular Grigori and was greatly relieved. I even hung around Austin until the summer heated up, relaxing and enjoying the youthful shenanigans of this fine city."

I absorbed the gentle burn of whiskey while I ordered my thoughts. Focusing on Smoke, I said, "After everything that's happened today, I have to believe what she says. So, you're part man, part god? That would explain some things."

Eirian distracted my gaze as she corrected me, "Not god, angel." I waited for her to go on. "According to Smoke, his father's father was an angel." She added, "My father was an angel." I felt like a Ranger again as the bombs kept falling. "Your father was an angel too."

"Now, wait a cotton-picking minute!" The waitress looked over. I gestured for another round, then resumed more quietly, "I never knew my father, but my mother told me he was a soldier."

Eirian's eyes were hooded, and she kept her voice low. "As far as that goes, she wasn't lying to you. All angels are warriors on one side or the other of a celestial war ongoing almost since the first soul came into being."

Smoke rumbled, "This I learned from my grandmother, and while that war has not involved me, I feel it coming."

Eirian swept the edge of her hand in a negating gesture. "We are all soldiers, no matter what we want."

Smoke's grunt sounded like assent. I shook my head. "I've done my stint in the Army. I'm just trying to make a living."

Eirian's laugh was not so musical this time. "Mr. Waite, you do not yet understand."

"Look, no matter what I do or do not get, this is pretty intimate stuff. Please, call me Harmon. Mr. Waite was my father's name."—I hesitated—"Or, at least, that's what my birth certificate says."

Eirian stared at me sternly but relented. "Harmon, you have a light in you. Darkness is all around. The Celestial Wars is an eons-old, inevitable fight between those two forces. Chaos and entropy will eventually overwhelm creation and order, and at the end of time, darkness will be the only truth in this Universe. Until then, life dances in the light." A sad smile touched her luscious lips. "Some are born to protect. As the son of an angel, your light shines brighter. One day, you will realize you have no choice."

I stared at my whiskey while the waitress delivered our second round. I waited until she was gone before I demanded, "Tell me about angels."

Smoke rumbled, "When I was a child, my mother used to share stories with me."

Smoke's deep tones grew more measured, like he was retelling an oft-heard tale. "God created angels, and the angels raised man above our ape ancestors. From his angelic roots, man dominated and spread throughout this world. Angels are tools of God's will, but free will is part of God's plan for Man. In elevating our race, some angels became invested and were corrupted.

"Man's free will was forbidden fruit. Over time and by association, those angels ate of that fruit. They gained knowledge of good and evil, which is at the heart of free will, and they rebelled against God's plan. Imagining they knew better, they bestowed their own creations with life.

"Those angels are the ones we call The Fallen, and their creations have, for the most part, become devils."

Eirian grimaced. "Unless that was part of God's plan too."

I gave her a sidelong frown, but Smoke barely paused. "The first generations of men were called Nephilim. Long-lived and full of light, many stayed on this Earth for a thousand years or more and boasted a measure of their angelic fathers' powers.

"For them, time was no prison, and the strength of their faith brought many miracles to pass. Their powers spawned legends, and for countless spans, the world was full of light. But even the long-lived must eventually pass to dust. As endless generations followed, the angel's essence, the power they had imbued in Man, became diluted. Today, humans are far closer to animals than angels."

Smoke's eyes had been half-closed while, perhaps because of his deep, rumbling bass, his tale raised the hairs on the back of my neck and resonated like faith in my heart. Now, he opened them and focused on me. "Although very rare, from time to time, in an act of creation, an angel still shares his seed with a woman. From those unions, men and women are born whose lights shine brighter than the rest of the human race. Of those few, fewer still exhibit the powers of the first humans, many of whom became known as gods themselves in the myths of ancient peoples."

Smoke finished his story, "That is why I have had premonitions involving you, Harmon Waite. Your light draws evil to you, as the darkness wrapped around him allows Eirian to track the one you call Jack."

Eirian added, "Just as it was his light allowed me to find Smoke from the other side of the veil." She leaned back and put both hands on the table. "Harmon, when I first saw your light, I understood I had discovered another angel's son, a joy I have not had the pleasure of since the last World War."

I looked from Smoke back to Eirian when she spoke and tried to steady my thoughts. "Eirian, the fact that you've seen the horrors of WWII is harder to take than Smoke's story of a human race created by angels instead of God. Maybe it's because I'm having trouble reconciling the beautiful, young woman I see in front of me with the seasoned warrior I hear talking."

I held up my hands as Eirian frowned. "I was raised in Texas, where women are appreciated and protected, but not typically warriors. Just give me a bit to finish absorbing." An ember of Eirian's smile sparked back to life, delighting me. "I have a bunch of questions, and I don't know how much I can buy into this whole there's a bright light inside me line of thinking, but only one of them is urgent—How do we stop Jack the Ripper before he murders again?"

Chapter 9 – Attack of the Hellhounds

Eirian said decisively, "We burn the body. This time we don't take any chances. We behead and burn."

I said, "It sounds like this devil can jump from one place to another. If we burn him, won't the Grigori just turn to smoke or whatever he does?"

Eirian replied grimly, "That's where my blade comes in. Major injuries inflicted by a blessed blade steal a devil's power, so he shouldn't be able to evade his fate." She looked thoughtful, then added, "To be safe, I will remove Jack's head this time. Devils are as long-lived and hard to kill as we are, but he won't make it back to Hell if we can end him with sufficient finality on this plane. It will take longer than the life he has left to return to our world again if he does. He's not that powerful, after all."

I shuddered and rubbed my badly bruised shoulder. "Not that powerful?"

Eirian clarified, "You encountered Jack in Purgatory, which is nigh unto Hell. He's close to invulnerable there. Jack is nasty, but he's not all-powerful, not even unique, just the most well-known in today's world out of his pack of nearly two hundred.

"As a whole, they are called The Grigori, but they are incubi—predators that tempt or force people to have sex with them. Spawned over the ages by the fallen angel, Yeqon, like other creatures, they possess diverse character traits. Jack has devolved into a sexually obsessed murderer. His love of sharp blades and taunting ways, everything about him arises from his delight in creating a sense of helpless horror meant to engender extreme fear in his victims."

"Lovely," I muttered. "So, how do we find this misbegotten devil again?"

"As I said, he's drawn to your light. That girl was killed close by, wasn't she?"

"Yes, outside the club Smoke and I were sitting in. It's right up the street.

Smoke held up a hand. "She is not deceased." We looked at him in disbelief. "She was badly injured, but I have a little talent. I mended the damage to her stomach."

Eirian looked at Smoke, the wonder back in her eyes. "An angel's son, and an angel's grandson who is a healer, both in one night. I am surely blessed."

Intense emotions roiled through me, but all I said was, "Thank you, Smoke."

Smoke shrugged. "I believe that means your devil is both angry and hungry."

I turned to Eirian. "Won't your sword have weakened him?"

"Not in Purgatory. There, he is not so bound by the laws of our mortal plane. Purgatory is his playground, Harmon. Even my blessed blade might not have allowed us to survive if you had not brought your power to bear when you did."

Smoke grew as still as the mountain he resembled. "Evil is coming. I believe Jack knows we are here." Eirian looked toward the south in alarm, uttered a curse in French, and stood, drawing her blade. Alarm bells went off in my head an instant before the front door exploded inward. Two massive, barrel-chested, coal-black canine forms hurtled through the ruined opening.

I glimpsed huge fangs and glowing red eyes as I pushed away from my chair and pulled my Colt. My adrenaline rush kicked the room into slow motion, and I blurred toward the front window looking for a clear shot. The larger of the two hounds focused flame-filled eyes on me. In one enormous bound, the beast crossed the space between us. Happily, that gave me a clear trajectory. I fired up and away from everyone—into the leaping hellhound's face.

My first shot tore a hole in its throat. My second ripped into its jaw, and a black mist sprayed as one ivory fang spun away. My third shot went down its gullet. As the beast rocketed past me, I twisted to one side, and massive jaws clamped on thin air. It skittered to a stop, adding deep claw marks to the already scarred wood floor.

The hellhound slid to a stop, shook its head, then whipped around. I was already standing over it, discharging bullets at its broad skull. That didn't slow the beast. It snapped at the gun in my hand, and I kicked upward, catching it under the jaw. The beast's fangs ground together as its head jerked back.

With preternatural clarity—time still crawling—I pumped hollow points into its center mass. The beast reared, came down on all fours, and howled with rage. I reloaded as I backpedaled, and it charged again. Even in hyper-speed, its assault from so short a distance left me feeling well and truly screwed.

The hellhound came for my throat, and I did the only thing I could. I stuck my pistol through those gaping jaws and emptied my new clip. The hound jerked its head violently, tearing ragged holes in my bomber jacket, knocking the .45 from my hand. Its bulk crashed into me, and as we both collapsed to the floor, the overwhelming smell of rotten eggs assaulted my nostrils. I watched the red flames flicker and go out from less than a foot away as the hellhound's weight faded into a pall of shadows.

Flopping onto my belly, I saw Eirian sheathe her sword and watched as another flicker of shadows rose toward the low ceiling. Smoke stood there, a sawed-off shotgun small in his hand. He was shaking his head, so I thought it likely he hadn't been able to find a clear shot.

The bartender and waitress stood frozen. She looked puzzled, like she simply couldn't grasp what had happened. He was probably wondering where the big dogs had gone, maybe assessing the damage. There wasn't much. My mangled hollow points lay on the floor where the hound had disappeared. I scooped them and the spent cartridges up as Smoke's shotgun vanished under his duster. As she sheathed it, Eirian's sword did the same.

The front door was hanging on one hinge, and the wooden frame had been twisted. Eirian walked over to the bar, dropped five one-hundred-dollar bills in front of the bartender, then placed another hundred on the young girl's textbooks. She spoke with quiet authority. "I am sorry for the evil visited upon your establishment this night. If someone reported the shots and the police show up, I recommend silence versus a trip to Bellevue." She gave them a ghost of a smile, then led us through the broken doorway and out into a far more menacing night.

If the police did show up, I figured those two would be hard-pressed to explain that front door, but it could have been worse. We had put innocents in the line of fire. *Never again*, I silently promised myself. *Never again.*

Pulling rear guard duty as we headed toward Smoke's Hornet, I suddenly remembered how good it had felt to have a team around me. *Brotherhood of warriors*, my heart whispered hopefully in my chest. A couple of folk who had been strangers a few hours ago felt like family. If anyone was the rookie, it was me. With some satisfaction, I thought, *We are all coming for you, Jack.*

Chapter 10– Harmon Goes to Hell

As we piled into the roomy front seat of the Hudson, I asked an obvious question, "Do you both think Jack sicced those hellhounds on us?"

Eirian shrugged. Smoke's answer was succinct, "Yes, Harmon Waite."

I had to wonder. Was this still a hunt for a lone serial killer? Eirian had said The Ripper was one of a pack of two hundred devils. If light and darkness are both discernible and compelling to celestial folk, could we already have drawn other devils to us? And, what of their master, Yeqon?

I shrugged, deciding *Sufficient unto the night*, replaced the empty clip in my Colt with my final spare, and made sure my knife was snug in its sheath. We cruised past The Continental Club heading south on Congress. No one was in sight, and no threat materialized. Smoke U-turned at Mary Street, and a sense of foreboding, like the pressure of an oncoming storm, drew us back toward the crime scene.

As we drove past the club again, I stared into the dark maw of the alley that had taken me to Purgatory. Yellow police tape hung limp, and the flashing lights from the police cruisers reflected redly against the brick walls, but nothing threatened.

Evil was close, and I wasn't the only one feeling it. Eirian murmured, "Smoke, take the next right."

Smoke turned, and his big automobile rolled along a narrow two-lane road behind the club. A line of half-height dumpsters, like the one at the rear of Threadgill's, lined the right side. I asked Smoke to stop, then stepped out, feeling a shuddering premonition. The backsides of the buildings where the dumpsters squatted were full of forlorn shadows. The breeze picked up—carrying with it a metallic smell. Blood.

I lifted the lid of the nearest trash canister. Nothing. I moved upwind, checking the dumpsters as I went. The third dumpster had a body in it, splayed across a pile of cardboard boxes. It was an older woman, her plain cotton shift hiked up to her chest, a deep slash spilling her entrails over the red wrinkles of her stomach.

Smoke and Eirian were out of the vehicle, and we all felt Jack's evil presence. Wary but angry, I paused to recite an intercession over the woman's corpse. "Incline Thine ear, O Lord, as I humbly pray Thee to show Thy mercy upon the soul of Thy servant, whom Thou hast commanded to pass out of this world. Place her near peace and light, and bid her be a partaker with Thy Saints. Through Christ, our Lord. Amen."

Another mangled corpse, a forever image, built the tally for retribution's sake. Jack was too strong, too in control, and we were stuck in his murderous web. Somehow we had to change the rules of his vicious game.

A faint shimmer at the back of the dumpster caught my attention. Before I could react, a massive arm emerged from thin air, grabbing the front of my jacket—lifting and jerking me hard into the dumpster—slamming my knees painfully against its metal lip.

Dragged across the woman's corpse, I was flung through a shimmering space by greater-than-human strength. Even as I fell, I shouted, "Light!" and a blessed silver glow sprang to life. Tucking my body, I hit Purgatory ground rolling. As I came to my feet, a fist like a wrecking ball slammed into my head.

The world swam out of focus while a coarse voice gloated in my ear. "Tiny human, it's time to play with Jack." The Ripper wrapped an enormous arm around my neck. He smelled as bad as a befouled corpse, and I gagged as I choked.

His harsh chant made no sense but etched my bones as flame corrodes wood. I felt more than saw us pass through another gate. Then Jack dumped me to the ground. I had half a heartbeat to wonder where we were before the howling of the damned filled my ears.

***

Evil washed over me like a tsunami. Cries of overwhelming agony raised my unwilling head, and I looked around and around. Gremlin-sized devils were torturing an endless sea of people. Every single one—young, old, man, woman—were sobbing, moaning, screaming victims of vicious abuse.

I saw one tiny devil stab an obese woman in her jelly-like rear with an iron poker. Her flesh rippled, contorting away from the pain, and she screamed—a wild, hopeless, piercing wail. Rage built in my chest—only to be subsumed by disbelief as the ugly wound healed at an impossible pace. Flesh mended, agony dissipating as her body recovered, the fat woman's screams became moans.

Another pint-sized devil sidled up behind and viciously shoved a smoking brand into the fat woman's hairy crotch. She caught fire and could not reach below the rolls of her stomach to extinguish the flames. Flesh burning, her mouth opened wide in a rictus of a scream. Then blackened flesh turned a healing pink. Her red thatch grew back, curling into a thick mass, and her mouth relaxed.

Dead eyes locked on another devil as he danced up to her and, without apparent effort, plucked her eyes from her skull. Her head wobbled madly as she fought the sudden dark. Covering her empty eye sockets with trembling hands, she begged for mercy.

The devil listened with canted head. He studied the situation, snapped his fingers, pried open her mouth, and took her tongue. He went on to pull out her fingernails and break her fat fingers.

Even as her body started healing, I turned away from that grotesque theatre and was confronted by an endless vista of torture and defilement that ran like a sea of grief out to the red horizon. A dreadful reality, it was tended by tens of thousands of dwarfish devils—the damned abused, given respite, then made to endure worse. The suffering of countless souls washed over me in a parade of pain.

My brain stumbled toward the safety of madness. As though he sensed I was on the edge, Jack reached down, picked me up, and shook me until my teeth rattled. "Wake up, wake up, little man. Don't go away. We are just getting started. There are six more stops on our sweet tour of Hell." He laughed gleefully, as enthused by the carnage as I was sickened.

More scenes like this to come?

I croaked, "No more," but we were in the seat of his power. Jack scooped me carelessly over his shoulder and trotted through the chamber, every so often pausing to stroke flesh that shrunk madly from his touch. Somewhere along the way, abused senses overloaded, I passed out.

I awoke to a different horror. I could hear cries of pleasure that sounded like pain. Sluggishly uncramping my mind, I looked around. A garish blue light suffused the scene, illuminating a bleak landscape of tumbled boulders, jagged rocks, and a strewn tangle of men and women.

For as far as I could see, on blocks of stone and clear patches of ground, individuals were engaged in every kind of sex. Jack knew I was awake and taunted me with undisguised delight, "You know they can never stop. They can't eat, can't sleep. These miserable creatures have an itch they can't scratch, and the need to keep trying drives them to the edge of sanity. There is no escape. They have an eternity to degrade and be degraded. It's a grand loop of their misspent lives."

I saw devils, large and small, scattered throughout the chamber. They all had thick phalluses and were using them indiscriminately on every hole of every human there. Jack was in ecstasy.

"You see? There, and there, and there? I do believe I can ensure my embraces are even more loathsome than those wretched excesses. So much pleasure, so much pain, and all of it so much fun. This is undoubtedly the grandest chamber in Hell!

"I leave you now, little man. Partake if you like. I am sure you have seen—these human damned are in the bloom of eternal youth. No matter your taste, beauty aplenty is here. Give in and give them a try. One and all, they want you."

Jack left me lying there, and as I looked upon that mockery of human need, my shock and horror gave way to anger—a deep sense of wrongness overrode the terrible despair eating at my soul. This twisting of one of life's sacred joys into warped travesties of lovemaking was not meant for living eyes. My righteous rage overwhelmed my hurting heart.

I. Do. Not. Belong. Here!

I lost myself in prayers. Hail Mary, followed by the Lord's Prayer. The scene's meaning faded as those blessed words took hold of my bruised and aching brain. My faith's comfort filled my consciousness, and I felt a familiar electric hum burn along my nerves. A wash of white radiance spread from where I knelt, infuriating the nearest devils—who started toward me with spits and howls.

I invoked another prayer to Christ and felt my body become pure light. An intense beam of concentrated energy flowed from above, meeting my own light—enveloping me, body, mind, and soul. Before that horrible vision of Hell faded, I could see every human and devil in the chamber still their ceaseless motion, all eyes turning toward me. The devils began shrieking with fear and rage, and the humans cried out, supplicating or cursing. Jack looked up from his buggering. I dimly heard his scream of incoherent fury, and smiled.

A gentle universe carried me from that cursed inferno of eternal suffering—back to the sweet coolness of the Austin night.

Chapter 11 – A War Council

I don't know how, but I was standing next to my BMW. I glanced down. My clothes were a mess, but I didn't hurt. That holy light had healed my worst injuries. More, my mind was calm and clear. Some divine power had pulled me from Hell's embrace, mended body and soul, then delivered me back to my vehicle. Even the memory of that place felt like background noise against the peace in my heart.

I wondered if the entire experience would continue to fade, or become vivid again once I was over my shock. I shuddered, knowing which I preferred. Unzipping the glasses pocket of my bomber jacket, I drew out my keys and drove around the corner to the rear of the club again.

As if mere moments had passed, Smoke and Eirian were still next to the dumpster. Maybe I hadn't been there as long as it felt, or perhaps Hell existed outside of time? I gave up on the thought before it went anywhere. I was still wrapped in the calm center of my faith, but I didn't quite feel up to contemplating the nature of eternity.

Stopping behind Smoke's Hornet, I stepped out, and my tranquil heart embraced my new friend's joy. When they demanded to know what had happened, I invited them to my house, promising I would explain everything.

I wasn't stalling—I needed the drive to gather threads of further thoughts. I would tell the story of my trip to Hell, and they could believe it or not as they chose, but the calm, sure power bathing my mind demanded a council of war. I had a plan to end Jack the Ripper before he could murder another innocent, and that's what I really wanted to share.

A few blocks from home, I made a quick stop at a public phone booth next to the road and called 911 to report another dead woman in another dumpster. Although I kept the call short, I figured if Molly listened to the recording, I'd be in even hotter water with her. I hung up before the officer could start asking questions, then thought about reaching out to Noble. The old man might still be up, but it was getting on toward midnight, and we were only one day into the investigation. Unsure what to say that he'd believe, I decided to phone him in the morning.

A few minutes later, I gratefully pulled into my driveway, and we headed into the house. Grabbing a couple of beers from the fridge, I set them on the dining room table and begged patience. Hopping into and out of a cleansing shower, I threw on another pair of jeans, a long-sleeve t-shirt, and sneakers. Thoroughly refreshed, I placed another round of beers on the table and sat opposite Smoke.

Looking back and forth between him and Eirian, I exhaled, took a sip, then recounted my trip to Hell. A mantle of clarity still protected me from the insanity I'd witnessed. I felt the horror once removed, stayed focused on the facts, summarizing, not graphically describing Hell. Both concentrated on my face intently and didn't interrupt.

When I finished, Eirian shook her head. "That shouldn't be possible. You can't go to Hell in a physical body."

I responded with the same conviction that had brought me out of Hell, "I damned—excuse me—darned well knew I didn't belong there, but I **was** there."

Smoke and Eirian gave me long, thoughtful stares, then looked at each other. Finally, Smoke volunteered, "He is one with the Force. Good!"

I snorted. Eirian shook her head. "From here to Hell and back. That's not a journey I could or would ever want to make. I still have to doubt Jack transported your mortal form there, but..." she trailed off, regarding me seriously, "Harmon, I wish I knew who your father was. He must be a mighty angel."

I shrugged. "The only thing I care about is whether he gifted me with enough of whatever these strange powers are to take out Jack before he kills again." I paused, considering my next words. "And I think I know how to do that." Both warriors gave me their full attention. "I only have one question. Are there gates to Purgatory all over this world?"

Eirian responded without hesitation, "Portals between worlds lie at nexus points along lines of power. Austin is at the intersection of multiple lines, so gates cluster thickly throughout this entire region."

I smiled, "That's good, albeit scary news." I filed the implications for future reference and focused on what it meant for my plan. Pushing away from my chair, I began pacing the table's length. "Hear me out. I've been at Jack's mercy on his home turf, and I escaped. The last time I saw him, The Ripper was one pissed-off devil. I have to believe he's already on his way, and I want to use that. Zilker Park is empty this time of night. If we can make it that far, there won't be anyone else for him to attack while he's trying to take me down."

A sudden pounding on my front door interrupted us. I tensed, then relaxed and asked the room, "If that's Jack, do you think he'd knock?" I smiled at my own poor joke. "Stay here and stay ready. I think I know who it is. You're not in any danger, but you'll want to be on guard." I went to the front door, opened it, and told my oldest friend in the world, "Molly O'Sullivan, what a pleasant surprise."

Molly looked more than annoyed. "Can it, Harmon! I'm on the second half of a double shift. I'm investigating both an attempted murder and a murder. A homeless woman was killed in a dumpster—again!" She added almost plaintively. "I can see the morning headlines." Pausing, she squinted at the bruises purpling my face. "Jeez, Harmon, what have you been doing, wrestling bears?"

"It's been a busy day."

She grunted and pushed her way inside. "Good, I hope it's been a productive one."

I sidestepped the question as I stepped aside. "Come on into the dining room, Molly. I have some associates I want you to meet." Molly hesitated, so I led the way. I introduced Smoke and Eirian. Smoke stood politely. Eirian had the hint of a smile like she already knew what was coming.

I explained they were helping me with the investigation. Molly smiled back at Eirian doubtfully, then looked Smoke up and down. "They reported a large Native American male at the scene of my attempted murder tonight. The name he gave was"—she pulled a notepad out of her jacket pocket and riffled through the pages—"Smoke on Distant Mountain." She paused. "The report also mentioned he was a medic in the military and was doing an excellent job treating the victim's wounds when officer"—she looked at her notes again—"Charles Alvarez and his partner arrived at the scene. They let him continue to care for the woman until an ambulance arrived."

Molly looked at Smoke directly. "That young lady is still unconscious but in stable condition. The doctor treating her now says he'd like to talk with you, but the bottom line for me is, he believes you saved her life." Her smile was tired but sincere. "Thank you, Mr, um, Smoke." I grinned, knowing she'd bit her tongue on that one.

Smoke gave her a slow smile that reminded me of dawn's breaking light. "You are welcome, Detective Molly O'Sullivan. I am pleased to hear the young lady survived."

Molly frowned. "The report says you stated you came on the scene after the assailant fled?" There was an inquiring note in her voice.

"Yes, Detective O'Sullivan, that is correct."

Molly continued to frown. "How did you just happen to be there to help that girl?"

"I was down the street at another bar. The Continental Club seemed a good place to get a nightcap, maybe listen to some music."

Molly digested this, then gave us the once over, her green eyes going icy. "And now, here we all are." Daggers flew my way. "Although they happened two hours apart, The Continental Club was the scene of both crimes. Beyond the fact of the dumpsters, all three attacks have involved what appears to be a powerful man with a sharp razor-like blade. We have damned little more to go on at this point." She glanced at my companions, then focused on me, "So Harmon, spill the beans. There's more going on here than you're letting on. I want to know what y'all have found."

I shrugged with as much nonchalance as I could muster. "Nothing useful to you yet, Molly."

Molly leaned forward, challenging me across the table with mounting anger, "Nothing? How the hell did you get so beat up over nothing?"

I looked at her steadily. "Molly, right now, I'm just one tired detective. We don't have anything that means anything to you. If I do come up with something solid, anything at all, I will call you asap."

The cold, hard light in Molly's eyes turned steely. "Harmon, let me be the judge of what is useful and what is not."

"No." the word was simple but absolute. It hung in the thickening air with no place else to go. Molly was my best friend, but what I knew was too unbelievable. Even if she somehow trusted me, I'd have to stop short of telling her my plan, or she'd demand to go with us. If there were police in the area, Jack would have victims. I couldn't let that happen.

Molly looked hurt but bit her tongue. She glanced at Smoke and Eirian, then looked back at me, all spiffed up and ready to dance. "I suppose your new friends are going back out with you now?" I sighed and nodded. "I should hold you for obstruction, but the hell with you, Mr. Waite, and I will let myself out!"

I winced as Molly stomped out of the dining room. I followed, and she paused after opening the door, a pleading note in her eyes. We'd been friends for way too long for me to do this to her. My shoulders tightened toward an involuntary shrug, but I stopped myself. I knew my own eyes were still asking for understanding. I felt something between us break as she went out the door into a far more dangerous night than she could or should know.

I returned to the kitchen, stuffing my frustration into a pocket at the back of my heart. Smoke and Eirian were sitting, waiting expectantly. They seemed to know better than to waste time on sympathy. I growled, "You with me?" Both nodded their heads. "Then grab your weapons, and let's go dance with a devil."

My anger returned and redoubled, humming in my head like a march. Yeah, no time for anything—except the evil that was likely already on my trail. That was fine by me. I might not have an exact handle on how to end him, but I had faith. Jack the Ripper's string of murders ran across centuries. Tonight was the end of the road for him. That my father was an avenging angel, I now had no doubt. I could feel his blood demanding justice.

As we headed south on Lamar in Smoke's Hornet, no one noticed the dark sedan following a couple blocks back.

Chapter 12 – Battle at Zilker Park

It was almost 4 a.m. by the time we made a right onto Barton Springs Road and slipped past the deserted patio festooned with metal umbrellas that nestles next to—providing outdoor seating for Shady Grove, one of the best burger joints in town. Crossing over the Barton Springs bridge, we parked at the closed entrance to the southern side of Zilker Park.

We crossed the road on foot, following a concrete path gleamed like a silver thread in the waning moon's light. It wound around the park's north side, and we moved at a trot until we reached its midpoint. Not far away, the Colorado River was a shambling dinosaur's ghost implacably pushing its way through the city. Hunkering down, I cleared my mind, ordering my thoughts and beginning the now comfortable process of gathering light.

Smoke was a steady presence on my right. Eirian stood on my left, Dyrnwyn in hand. At odds with her youthful beauty, she exuded a seasoned warrior's calm, competent confidence. I waited, wondering if the incoherent rage I'd felt consuming Jack the Ripper back in Hell would hold to its purpose. The passing minutes dragged muddy footprints of doubt through my faith, but I ignored 'em. Either Jack would come, or he wouldn't.

The wind rustling the oaks barely disturbed the quiet. There was the faint creak of wood as the river plodded past a boathouse on the far shore. Ei spoke quietly but distinctly, "Jack is in the area."

But when the peaceful night was finally interrupted, it wasn't what I expected. Gunfire. Explosive concussions in quick, professional bursts of three. Then footsteps headed toward us. A familiar voice cursed, then screamed.

A yell was ripped from my own throat, "Molly!" I was running before I knew I was up. Time slowed, and Molly's next scream was muted by hyper-speed. I fairly flew. I wanted, needed to see Molly. Now!

It was as if the moon had suddenly been made full. The increased radiance clearly revealed two forms, one on the ground, the other standing over.

The razor held a lingering gleam as it descended in slow motion, arcing toward Molly's throat. Even in my accelerated state, I knew I was out of time. I shoved my right hand out, willing hot light toward The Ripper. Concentrated energy erupted from my palm and slammed into Jack, staggering the big devil back before he could complete his murderous swing.

I wrapped my body in light and hit Jack the Ripper like a freight train. We both went to the ground rolling, my arms wrapped around his bulk. Wherever our bare skin touched, Jack burned. He screamed and pushed away from me with demonic strength.

Huge, Jack filled my vision as he leaped up and towered over me, his flesh sizzling—blackening patches flaking from his mottled hide. He swayed and twitched, his body jerking all over. It was unnatural and hideous. Almost as rhythmic as the ticking of a clock, he shivered, grimaced in pain, shuddered again. Cleared of shadows, Jack's features stretched gargoyle-like over bulging bones. He was already more twisted than any of the devils I'd seen in Hell, and his twitching stressed the wrongness of him, like a puppet wrapped in its own strings.

His black-beaded eyes radiated malevolence but something else as well. Jack took a step back, and I saw fear edging into his rage. I reached down to my ankle sheath and pulled my army blade. Time slid by sluggishly as I leisurely slashed Jack across the chest. Demon flesh shriveled, and black smoke curled from the wound. I cut at the arm holding the blade, and Jack dropped his straight razor with a croaking roar of mingled fury and fear. I slashed a third time as he took another step back, opening an ugly gash in his throat. His guttural growl became a gurgle.

Jack turned and ran.

I burned with the need to follow, but Molly came first. She lay on the ground gasping, a deep diagonal cut marring her police jacket. Thinking my desperate shot had been too little too late, I put my hands on either side with some idea of staunching the blood—and felt the rugged contours of a bullet-proof vest. Still frantic, I searched for other injuries, but Molly pushed my hands away gently, "Harmon, I'm ok."

I released the breath I didn't know I'd been holding. "Good. Good." I muttered inanely, mumbling a prayer of thanks as relief flooded my adrenaline-infused body.

Smoke and Eirian ran up as Molly struggled to a sitting position. She looked around. "What the hell was all that?" Molly paused, digesting what she'd seen. "And where'd the perp go? Damnit, let me up!" Focusing on me, her mouth dropped open. "Harmon, you're wearing a halo!"

There was nothing here to laugh at, but I couldn't help myself. I hadn't noticed the halo, and at that moment, it seemed way too stereotypical. Behind Molly, Smoke chuckled. Molly glared at us in annoyance as she rose to her feet. "What's going on here? I want answers."

I willed the God-light away and squinted up into the sky. The sliver of a moon swam there, barely lighting the night again with its thin radiance. "Well, ma'am, I do believe explanations are overdue. First, though…" I put her hand securely in mine and walked her over to where Jack and I had fought. At my direction, Molly clicked her flashlight on, and we all gazed down at the blade that had brought so much harm to so many.

Molly groaned, "So that was the murderer, and this is the murder weapon. I knew you were hiding something. I should have guessed you were going after the killer." She glared at me. "Harmon, you and your friends belong in jail, but dammit, you saved my life!" Her Irish ire fought with her heart and lost. "Harmon, just…thank you."

I made a shooing motion, and the ghost of a smile glimmered between us. Then, Molly frowned and, pulling a handkerchief from her pocket, stooped, wrapped the blade, and held it at arm's length. I figured she was wondering how many lives that makeshift weapon had stolen. She had no idea. I had a fleeting worry about what forensics would make of a blade from the 1800s, but there was nothing to be done now.

Molly sighed, slipping the evidence into her coat pocket, and turned to us. "None of this makes any sense. Y'all owe me a bunch of answers. There's a Kerbey Lane on Lamar. I'm buying. Make it worth my while."

I nodded. "Let's get out of here. Something still doesn't feel right." Smoke and Eirian's heads went up, their eyes automatically sweeping the area.

Even Molly looked around, then reproached me, "Enough of that, Harmon." I didn't say anything but stayed close enough to occasionally brush her shoulder as we headed at a steady trot back to our vehicles.

Chapter 13 – The Fight That Follows

Molly's cruiser was sitting next to the Hudson. I climbed in with her, and both vehicles headed back up Barton Springs Road. We'd crossed the low bridge over Barton Creek when a faint patch of lighter darkness off to the right caught my attention. "Molly, stop!" I said with more force than required. Molly jammed on the brakes, screeching to a halt. On our right, a two-lane road branched off toward a wooded area. Maybe thirty yards from us, a shimmering portal hung semi-transparent, ghostly in the dark.

Climbing out, I pointed my forefingers at my eyes, then toward the otherworldly gate. As the Hudson eased off the road, I leaned back into the cruiser. "Molly, I'd prefer you stay here, but I know you won't. Please bring that with you, though." I indicated the shotgun locked upright to the dash. I could see questions in her eyes, but she grunted assent.

By the time the others gathered on my right, Molly had the cruiser off the street, and shotgun in hand, was on my left. Since everyone else was looking in that direction, it only took her a moment to make out the portal. She pointed the barrel of her weapon. "Harmon, tonight has already been stranger than any of your tall tales. Want to tell me what that thing is?"

"It's a gate, a door to another, much darker place. And it's open."

"Sooo"—she drew out the word as she absorbed the implications—"Is something coming through?" She sounded worried, and I couldn't blame her. I figured Jack had activated that portal to get here in the first place. The fact that it was still open didn't bode any good.

I glanced toward the warriors on my right. "Do we want to close it or take advantage and take the fight back to Jack?"

"Not on Purgatory ground," Eirian said immediately.

I considered the situation. "Well, Jack left the gate open. Why don't we give him a chance to come back through. If he's that mad, we take advantage. Eirian, cover the left flank, please. Smoke, will you go right."

Eirian spoke up, "Smoke, hold a moment. I have an idea." Hesitating, she glanced at Molly.

Molly shrugged, "In for a dime, in for a dollar." Eirian evidently knew that one, and her smile looked as good as it had a couple lifetimes, or was it only a few hours ago when we strode Purgatory ground. She threw her long silver hair over her left shoulder and, reaching over her right, drew her sword.

Eirian held her blade out, then indicated Molly's shotgun—gesturing for my friend to lay its barrel over her sword. Her eyes asked Smoke to do the same. The big Indian reached under his duster and drew his own shotgun out of hiding. My friend raised an eyebrow as he laid its short barrel on the sword next to hers.

Focusing on me, Eirian said, "Harmon, please bless our weapons." I stared skeptically. "I am serious, Mr. Waite. We can go into why later, but I believe it will make a difference."

Unwilling to argue, I shrugged, "Ok."

Pulling my own weapons, I held them lightly atop the others. My fascination with the Catholic Church's history recalled a blessing popes once conferred on war-bound royalty during the renaissance era. Bowing my head, I gathered the light of faith that permanently resides in my heart.

"By the Holy Father, I appoint you as another sword of the Holy See. May your hand remain firm against the enemies of the Holy See. May your right hand be lifted up, intrepid warrior, as you remove them from the earth, and may your head be protected against them by the Holy Spirit, symbolized by the pearly dove. In those things deemed worthy by the Son of God, together with the Father and the Holy Spirit. Amen."

Everyone echoed the amen, and a delicate light played over our weapons like a dance of ghosts. My gear grew warm, and I glanced around. Eirian looked pleased. Smoke gave me a smile that said he'd expected this. Molly's eyes were wide. I could see puzzle pieces falling into place for her. I felt my own face break into a grin.

The light faded, and Eirian sighed with satisfaction. "My sword, Dyrnwyn, is already a blessed blade, but if anything comes through that portal in the next few minutes, I believe you will find your weapons more effective." She paused, and her lips quirked. "I've only seen swords blessed. It looks as though the boon works equally well on guns."

Night continued to draw toward day. I figured dawn was less than an hour away. I was a bit concerned about traffic but hadn't seen or heard any. As I brought my God-light to life to illuminate the area, my cares and worries faded to certainty. This was right. We were right to be here.

Eirian moved off to my left. Smoke gravitated to my right, a mountainous man on noiseless feet. Molly seemed happy enough to stay by my side. "Harmon, you're glowing again," she whispered. I smiled in her direction but kept my eyes on a slight movement in the shining curtain. A gremlin-sized devil stuck its ugly head into our world. It was the same size as the ones I'd seen in Hell. Molly gasped as it burst out of the gate and ran toward the woods. Smoke's shotgun blast followed. If he hit it, he didn't do sufficient damage to slow the wee beastie.

In rapid succession, three much larger devils catapulted out of the portal and fled toward the trees. Their only uniformity was their grotesqueness. One had a head and body that reminded me of a pig. The other two were man-sized, but the piggy-looking devil was hulking big. Smoke's shotgun blasts followed each, but only the pig-devil screeched and fell. It rose, shook itself, and charged Smoke. He reloaded with practiced speed, and his next round took it full in the chest. The devil dissolved into greasy mists that hung in the air before dissipating.

Without warning, the portal winked out of existence. Smoke didn't hesitate. He let out a war whoop that would have done his ancestors proud and chased the remaining devils into the woods. I cursed and hurried after him. Smoke's long legs gave him too much advantage, and he faded into the night. I willed light to encompass the woods. In the distance, the devils wailed in distress, but Smoke was briefly visible again before he faded into the tree line. The two women were close on my heels.

As we entered the woods, Eirian veered left. Molly and I slowed to a walk. We were surrounded by a silent spectacle—ground and trees bathed in silent majesty by the God-light. About a hundred yards in, the diminutive devil surprised us, launching itself out of a tree onto Molly's back. Sharp talons slashed through her shirt and bounced off her armored vest. I spun, firing one of my newly-blessed bullets over her shoulder, taking the devil directly between its burning eyes. Molly's shotgun blast dissipated the rising smoke. She gave me a disgusted look. "Harmon, you just blurred. First, you light up. Now you blur."

I grinned humorlessly, "Just one more thing to explain."

"You got that, Jack." I winced. She peered around. "What's next big boy? And please don't disappear on me again."

"Keep close. My bad feeling's getting worse." Molly pulled a cartridge from her shotgun's bandoleer and replaced the spent one. As I mentioned previously, I always find it a good idea to pay attention to my intuitions. I practically had my ear to that inner ground now. We entered a clearing in the woods. Without any chance to warn her, I jerked Molly down, dropping with her. A shotgun discharged nearby, producing a deafening report. Pellets tattered the trees in front of us, and I called out, "Smoke?"

His deep, rumbling voice carried out of the shadows, "Got one, Harmon Waite." He formed up on the edge of the clearing—a more solid shape against the variegated shades of the God-lit night.

Eirian stepped out of the woods to our left, sword held low. "I eliminated another."

I helped Molly to her feet, then nodded the way we'd come. "We took out the last one, but it doesn't feel like we're done yet." Echoing my warning, what could only be hellhounds let loose a cacophony of howls from the direction of the road. They were a ways off but coming closer. Moments later, more baying erupted on our left flank.

Eirian gave me a bemused look, then said to no one in particular, "Having fun yet?" As if that were our cue, everyone flowed into a loose ring and faced the surrounding trees.

Molly muttered, "Oh well, coffee sounded like a good idea." The others chuckled.

Eirian said, "Jack is opening and closing two nearby portals. I believe he will keep sending nasty surprises our way until dawn."

I checked my watch. It was 6:41 am. "Get ready for a very long few minutes, then."

Hellhounds loped out of the woods on either side of the clearing. They still looked more like oversized wolves—except for the coal-red eyes. Displaying the same wolfish behavior, both packs rushed us simultaneously, and my world went abruptly slow-motion. My pistol made deep chugging sounds as the bullets, far more effective now, forcefully returned a handful of them to Hell.

Out of the corner of my eye, I saw two of the fire-eyed beasts converging on Molly. Her shotgun dissolved one into shadowy mists. The other was going to blindside her, so I tackled it. We hit the ground rolling—my gun arm hard against its throat to keep slavering fangs from my neck. The blade in my free hand slashed the hound's belly, and a sulfurous stench hit me as the creature fell into a hazy smudge against the brightening sky.

I bounced to my feet, and Molly's shotgun went off in my ear. I spun to see another cloud of mist dissolving and shook my head, trying to clear it. Faintly, I heard, "Damn it, Harmon, I almost took you out."

A hellhound leapt for Molly's throat, and even quagmired by real-time, I managed to block-tackle it. My Ka-Bar cut the creature's throat from ear to ear, and the hellhound shifted to smoke, then sluggishly dissipated.

Staggering back to my feet, I checked my companions. Eirian's sword sliced through a hellhound as if it wasn't there. Then, it wasn't. Smoke kept firing—steady booming retorts that rolled through the woods. With every shot, a hellhound dissolved into grey mists that drifted sluggishly upon the silvered light.

I caught the pattering of a hound's feet from behind, but Molly's shotgun shredded the hellhound before I could complete my turn. Really missing my flakey hyper-speed capabilities, I reloaded and began firing at three more hounds headed in our direction. One fell into a ruin of smoke. The other two kept coming.

Molly must have been out of shells because she pulled her pistol and took out one of the creatures with a three-shot cluster so rapid-fire it blurred into a single explosion. I hammered the second half of my clip into the last supernatural beast and watched it thin into nothingness.

As day finally peeked over the world's rim, I searched but could see only blessedly empty clearing. "Anyone hurt?" Heads shook. "Then excuse me for saying this Molly, but let's vamoose before your police force friends show up."

Eirian gave Molly a sidelong look. "Devils can't manifest during the day, so we finally have time for that coffee." Molly nodded tiredly, and we returned to our vehicles as my God-light faded into daylight.

Chapter 14 – Coffee, Finally

We were being seated in Kerbey Lane Café when a cruiser flew by, lights on, sirens blasting. If the police searched the woods, I figured they'd find a few pellet-riddled trees and a few dozen shells. I thinly hoped they'd write it off as college kid hijinks.

Sipping my coffee, I contemplated the long and strange twenty-four hours had elapsed since I stood behind Threadgill's, viewing Jenny's corpse. That proved too exhausting, so I dug into my breakfast. Everyone else did the same. Smoke had two plates in front of him—trying out my favorite blueberry pancakes on one and regular flapjacks on the other.

Molly appeared to be as famished as the rest of us. I left her alone until her chewing slowed, then said, "Ok, Molly, I owe you an explanation."

"Or ten," she muttered around a mouthful. She looked thoughtful, swallowed, set her fork down, and said, "Let me save you some time, Mr. Waite. You've always been a bit strange, and my heart has trusted you anyway. Tonight, you saved my life, battled creatures straight out of a vision of Hell, handled light like it was yours to command, and moved faster than anything I've ever seen.

"I understand why you couldn't say something back at your house, and I'm sorry if I ruined the trap you set in Zilker for that murderous scum." She held up a pinky. "I'm not even quite sure you're human, but still friends?"

I wrapped my little finger lightly around hers and grinned, "Never any doubt."

"So, I know now that our killer definitely isn't human." She glanced around the table. "Why don't we start there."

I said, "Jenny Summers and that street person."

Molly interrupted, "Francis, her name was Francis McDermott."

I bowed my head, offering a short prayer for Francis's soul, then glanced around and lowered my voice. "Jenny and Francis were both murdered by a supernatural entity—a devil. He's one of a gang of fiends known as the Grigori. Devils have been interfering in our lives since the first humans walked this planet." I looked to Eirian for confirmation. She nodded but kept munching, leaving it up to me how much to tell my friend. Molly's tough as nails and smarter than most. I intended to tell her everything. "The modern world knows this particular devil as Jack the Ripper."

Molly choked on her coffee. "You've got to be kidding! No, never mind. Keep going."

"It's just a name. I'm sure he's been called others. The thing is, I pissed him off royally." Molly raised an eyebrow. I shuddered involuntarily as I replied to her unspoken question, "We've actually had a couple of run-ins. I've literally been to Hell and back with Jack." I held up a hand as she opened her mouth. "It gets stranger. Let me finish."

"According to Eirian and Smoke, I am the son of an angel." I rushed on as Molly frowned and set her cup down. "Now, I don't know that for a fact, but these two"—I indicated my colleagues with a wave of my hand—"have some peculiar powers of their own, and they tell me that my capabilities, like manipulating light and time, come from being an angel's child."

I paused, then took the plunge. "They also told me the human race was initially birthed by angels." I glanced over at my compatriots again. "It's just a more recent parentage for the three of us."

"God's more the Architect. Angels are the agents of His Will." Eirian threw in around a mouthful of pancakes.

"Not so much a concept, as an execution difference from what the Bible tells us?" Molly asked, delicately scratching the side of her nose.

Eirian looked pleased. "Exactly. But, if you dig deep enough into the Bible and holy texts in general, the meaning of much of what is written blurs. It's never as neat and clean as it's taught. There's even a name for the children of angels in the Bible. We are called Nephilim." I remembered the term from Smoke's explanation earlier and made a mental note to look it up later.

Taking up the story again, I said, "Bottom line, Jack passes back and forth to our world through the same kind of gates you saw those devils use, but he can only be harmed on the mortal plane. Since he has a big hard-on against me, we wanted to lure him into a fight in a place that would avoid collateral damage."

Molly said, "That explains why you did what you did, and I apologized." She hesitated, struggling with her cop instincts—"So, what do we do now?"

Before she could have second thoughts and decide she was breaking too many rules, I said decisively, "We figure out another plan of attack before darkness rolls around and Jack comes visiting again. There are two points in our favor." I stuck up a couple fingers. "One, Jack appears to be attracted to us three in particular, since our hearts, souls, or whatever it is lights us up shines differently." I left the statement hanging and glanced over at Eirian again.

"Much brighter soul lights," she confirmed. Then, true to her teacher's nature, she ensured she was clear as mud by wiping her lips with a napkin and pointing at her heart.

I started to go down that rabbit hole but stopped myself just in time. I could swear there was a faint glimmer of a smile under the weary lines on Eirian's elfin face. Instead, I took my first finger down, left my middle finger up, and with a savage grin, said, "And, two, like I said, Jack is royally pissed off at me."

Molly looked back and forth between Eirian and me. Finally, she grabbed my finger and squeezed firmly, giving me a hard stare. "This devil, who heaven help us is Jack the Ripper, is hard to kill? Are those blessed weapons we used tonight going to do the job?"

Eirian's shoulders twitched, but she answered for me, "Unknown. Maybe. If we can do sufficient damage."

I said, "My blessed pistol was definitely more effective against those hellhounds than against the one in the bar earlier." Before Molly could ask, I explained, "We had a run-in with a couple of those oversized canines up the street from The Continental Club. There wasn't much damage, and no one was hurt."

Molly reproached me silently as Eirian shrugged and suggested, "I do think it worthwhile to obtain the most effective weapons we can and bless them before the sun goes down. Shotguns are probably best. Their damage is greater, and the range limited, which minimizes collateral casualties. We need other weapons, though. Ones that do not run out of ammo. Does anyone know how to use a sword?"

Molly promptly spoke up, "Yes." Smoke and I looked at each other, then shook our heads.

Eirian asked, "Do you have a melee weapon you're comfortable with?"

Smoke nodded. I thought about it. "Besides my knife, no."

Eirian shrugged noncommittally. "That will have to do. If I find something else for you, I'll bring it."

I said, "Can we meet at my house around 4 pm? That should keep you out of rush hour traffic." Everyone was agreeable. I turned to Molly. "Can I get a ride with you back to my place? That'll give me a chance to answer the forty thousand other questions on your mind." Molly nodded, pleased. I looked around the table as we stood. "One more thing, dress for rough country."

We hugged on the way out. It was an angel thing. Molly and I both climbed into her cruiser, and I answered questions on the way back to my house. She was too sharp to doubt her own eyes, but I think she was still wrapping her head around the idea that her old friend was someone other than whom she'd always thought him to be.

Mercifully, she simply dropped me off when we got there. I didn't even stop to shower. Dropping into bed, I immediately fell into a deep, albeit not dreamless sleep.

Chapter 15 – Gusion The Seer

The dream wasn't just a dream. I was standing in a field of golden grass under the bluest sky I'd ever seen. Fluffy cumulus clouds floated lazily across heaven's vault like sailboats on a summer's day. In front of me stood a fallen angel. I knew he was Fallen because his terrible wretched beauty twisted my soul and stopped my heart. Limbs of alabaster perfection were as pearly white and cleanly rounded as the clouds. His hair was long and startlingly blue. And he gazed at me with amber eyes—the same distinct, brilliant gold as the grasses.

When I stared into them, those molten eyes rippled and became a fathomless ocean of gold so deep I fell in but never reached bottom—drowned and never knew I was lost. An eternity passed. I was content in a silence one degree removed from my mortality. When he finally shattered the stillness, his words chimed and swirled like notes of sunshine, "Your name is Harmon Waite." My mind began the slow climb back to self-awareness. "I am Gusion. I am here to help you."

"Why?" I got the one word out—my voice as hoarse as wind falling down a deep cavern's mouth.

"Do you know me?"

I shook my head, still not trusting my voice. With the barest hint of sadness, he said, "I know more pasts and futures than have ever been. I am not omniscient, but I am blessed to understand you have a role to play in our war."

Trying for coherent thought, I ground out a question, "War, what war?"

"The war for Heaven and Earth. The one war that eons from now will become the death of the Universe. A war with many battles to be won or lost between now and that end of time."

He stopped. Still entranced, I said, "I thought devils were ugly." Gusion laughed. It boomed like thunder and ran round and round inside my head. When I could think again, I said, "What do you want from me?"

"Only to answer your questions and give you a gift."

I couldn't help myself. "Are you my father?"

Gusion laughed that same mind-bewildering laugh. A line from an old novel crawled through my head, The merriment of the gods is not for mortal ears. "No, Harmon Waite, I am not your father, but I know your father. He would take great interest in learning that your light has begun to outshine your self."

"Who is my father?" If I could find that out, I might start to figure out my place in a world spawned angels and devils with equal abandon.

"You will know your father soon enough, but not today," Gusion replied negligently.

A faint annoyance flickered against the back of my mind, like the barest trace of heat lightning. It was just enough to help me regain equilibrium. "What answers do you have for me, then?"

"I can tell you how to stop the one you call Jack."

I resisted the surge of hope. "Why would you do that?"

A storm cloud hung its purple lining over his brow. "Because Jack is dangerous. His hungers threaten the balance between your world and the heavens. We have worked long to bring man to our light. Earth is on the cusp. Yeqon and his Grigori would drag humanity back into the darkness, where fear of what is in and under the heavens ruled your lives."

"If that's true, why don't you stop him." I felt my anger spark into a flame. The dream fell out of focus. Everything dimmed.

Gusion made the slightest motion with his left hand. The entire landscape glowed more brightly for an instant, then stabilized, and was again as sweet and sure as new love's face. "Careful, Harmon Waite. You do not yet know how to control your power, and we still have more to do before I give you back to self and sleep." He frowned at me, the gentlest of rebukes. "Stopping these murders has been gifted to you by your fate. If you succeed, you may find a life worth living. If you do not, it will not matter. You will be lost in the kingdoms of the dead."

I tamped down my anger. "Then, tell me about my powers. How do I control them?"

"Your will," Gusion replied with effortless, perfect simplicity. "If it is your will, and it is within your power, it will be. That is your gift from your father."

For a moment, it seemed that was all the answer he would give. Then, the fallen angel continued in a different voice. As if pronouncing judgment, he said, "All you need is a focus for your will. For that, I have a gift."

Gusion reached his left hand into my chest. It happened so suddenly I didn't have a chance to draw back. Light blossomed from my heart. Like a thermal explosion, it went silver-white, overwhelming my dream vision. I felt something vital go out of me. I couldn't say precisely what, but when I could see again, Gusion held a small globe of light. His other hand reached into his own breast. He drew from it another ball, more of lightning than light.

He brought both hands together precisely, and the two orbs merged. His fingers flew, blurring as they crafted with the delicate speed of an angel in the act of creation. Even as the form became apparent, he finished and handed a katana-like sword to me without flourish.

Awed by its elegance, I turned the blade over and over. A single-sided sword, it sported the same black finish as my Ka-Bar. It was three feet long and had a leather-wrapped hilt I effortlessly grasped first one, then two-handed. The leather was warm, and I could swear it pulsed faintly.

A celestial sword forged by an angel, it already felt like an extension of my own body, and I appreciated the extraordinary nature of his gift, but was confused. "Thank you, Gusion, but I don't have the faintest idea how to use a sword."

Gusion smiled again. "I pulled it more from your mind than your earth's history. It is what your companion would call a blessed blade. More than that, I have used the Creator in both of us to imbue this weapon with a life of its own. It will help you in ways an ordinary blade cannot. It is linked to you. Its purpose will become clear upon need."

I kept my thoughts to myself, but Gusion divined what I was not saying. "Yes, I am a fallen angel, one of those who is not afraid to create more than was originally Willed. I am also a seer of the angels. I know the place where your future meets your fate, and this sword will help get you there. Its name is Yeshu'a. It will be true to you."

He paused, then said, "We are done here, Harmon Waite. I send you back to your sleep. When you meet that Grigori again, make sure you have Yeshu'a by your side."

Gusion sensed my need and remained—as sure a presence as my own heartbeat. I hesitated, then spoke, "I have heard a thing that contradicts my faith. Will you please tell me who fathered the human race?"

Gusion smiled. "We angels are the caretakers of life in the Universe. When it was but newly formed, Abaddon carried the dust of this planet to God. God breathed life into that dust. God is the Father, but Abaddon brought that blessed dust to the angels and we architected the creatures of your world, from the greatest to the smallest—according to God's Will."

Gusion paused, then added reverently, "I will tell you that man is special. Spirits abound in this Universe, but it is a rare event, even in eternity, that angels are given the command to leave a divine spark, a small piece of God's soul—to grow in the beings they've created."

Gusion considered me. I stared back, no longer intimidated by his eyes' rippling, golden depths. When he spoke again, a musing note was in his voice, "It was also an angel who created Jack and his brothers."

He smiled at my obvious disgust. "Jack and the Grigori are Yeqon's children. What he conceived was outside God's plan, but the temptation to create and the responsibility for one's creations are separate matters. Yeqon does not see, but I have seen. Jack and his brothers would bring Hell to Earth. Hell is an end, not a means. They do not recognize that.

They only see their own need to feed, and they love to feed on fear which, as you are too well aware, should be Hell's exclusive providence."

I shuddered. "You know about that?"

"I am Gusion."

I had nothing else to ask. I looked down, enjoying the heft and refinement of the weapon. I was wondering how to get my new sword from dream to reality when Gusion and his perfect world dissolved. I could still feel the oddly reassuring presence of Yeshu'a as I slipped gently into dreams of more mundane things than God, angels, and the fate of worlds.

Chapter 16 – Our Team Gathers

I slept like a rock until mid-afternoon, then rolled out of bed, picked up my phone, and dialed Noble Summers. He answered on the second ring. "Harmon, where the hell have you been? You alright?" he demanded.

"Sorry, Noble. Yeah, I'm fine. I chased our killer all night and just finished snatching some shut-eye. We're closer to taking him than yesterday. Not close enough for my liking, though. I am leaving again shortly, maybe for the evening, and wanted to give you a heads up before I head out."

His tone gentled, "What do you need, son? How can I help?"

There was no sword on my bed or beside it, only my knife on the nightstand. Picking it up, I unsheathed the blade, and while giving Noble a general update that skated carefully around the supernatural, idly flipped it end over end. It was only my trusty old knife. I finished by reporting, "I've recruited a couple of pros, and Molly is helping. The team is supposed to meet here"—I looked at my alarm clock—"within the hour. Noble, your daughter's murderer may be one mean S.O.B., but my team is better than good. We have the weapons we need. Everyone should be rested and ready to take up the hunt again."

Noble muttered, "Yeah, I read about that murder at The Continental Club in this morning's Statesman. The papers are calling him a serial maniac. They say the man who killed my Jenny and murdered that other woman is the same one who brutally attacked the young lady outside that club earlier. If so, he is one insane son-of-a-bitch." The old man paused, clearly torn between his need and his worries. "You got this, right son? I'd hate to see something happen to you, too."

I ignored his question. "Noble, I'll get back to you as soon as possible."

He got what I wasn't saying. "I know you will, son. Be safe out there. Take that monster down before he kills someone else's little girl."

By the time our team arrived, I was showered, shaved, and even had food on the table. It was only sandwiches, but there were plenty of them filled with various deli meats from my fridge. Eirian chewed delicately on a turkey and rye. Molly made appreciative noises as she consumed her sourdough and ham. I had the same. Smoke waded in, trying a little of everything. I passed a Shiner beer over to him and opened a bottle of wine for the women.

I let my team take the edge off their hunger, then said, "Let's see what else we have to chew on. As I see it, our main challenge is the Ripper's ability to shift between Earth and Purgatory. Those gates are Jack's escape routes. The question is, ctake that advantage away from him? Eirian, can you close a gate from a distance?"

"Yes, a gate is not a natural part of this world. I can rebuke it, which will close the gate quite quickly."

"Can you sense a gateway's location before it opens?"

Eirian set her sandwich down and took a small sip of wine as she considered her response. "Yes. Those gates don't open just anywhere. I can pinpoint gate locations in a given area if I have a chance to scout it first."

"Excellent!" I turned to the big Indian. He still had on both his duster and his implacable face. "Smoke, how about you, can you sense a gate the same way Eirian does?"

He spoke around his mouthful of sandwich, "Harmon Waite, I can tell when one is open, but it is only a general knowing, more akin to a foreboding."

I considered. "I had the same experience last night. It was more of a bad feeling than certain knowledge." Smoke grunted agreement. "So, it's up to Eirian to shut any portal The Ripper comes through, then up to the rest of us to stop Jack before he can open another."

Molly spoke up, "Harmon, from what you said on the way back to your place, Jack is weaker in this world and driven by his hunger while here. Can we bait a trap?"

I shook my head, "I don't like the bait we'd have to use."

"Since I am the one most likely to be the bait, neither do I." Her eyes were green ice. "But, if it keeps another woman from being murdered, I'll do whatever I must. That's my job."

I replied cautiously, "Molly, I don't want to diss you by saying no. But putting you, me, or any of us out to hang in an ill wind doesn't seem like a great idea."

Molly started to object but bit her lip when Eirian laid a hand on her arm and said, "I believe I can keep his exits shut long enough for us to stop Jack the Ripper."

Smoke turned to me, "We have not considered one thing. The last time he faced you, Jack ran. Rather than take us on directly, I expect he will send a force against us again."

A new tension sparked to life around the table. I grimaced, then snapped my fingers. "If Jack doesn't want to join the party, he'll still have to direct it." I turned to Eirian. "Are the portals congruent between worlds?" She nodded. "Then, if there's more than one gate in the vicinity, I can use my speed to surprise Jack in Purgatory. I'll try to manhandle him into our world, and if it gets too hairy, I'll disengage."

I stared at the dubious faces. "If Jack stands back and slings troops at us, do y'all see another option?" Frowns deepened, but no one suggested we abort. If we didn't take Jack down somehow, we all knew more innocent blood would be on our hands.

I shrugged, "Ok, we'll call that one a play-it-by-ear scenario and hope Jack's too invested in revenge to stay out of the fight." The room remained grimly quiet. I cleared my throat and plowed ahead. "Weapons check is our next order of business."

Molly frowned. I knew she was not about to go along with me taking on Jack alone, any more than I'd be willing to let her play the goat. She also knew no plan survives first contact with the enemy, and she was an opportunist. I let her wheels turn as I removed the sandwich tray from the table. I was an opportunist too. She grunted as she picked up the big bag she'd toted in with her. "I brought my gun collection and plenty of ammo." She opened it and placed a pair of 9mm Glocks on her side of the table, then put a Colt and a .44 Automag in the middle.

Smoke reached for the wicked big Automag. The Colt .45, with its grey finish and walnut grips, was an earlier version of my own pistol. Eirian fancied that one, picking it up and examining its action. "I used one very much like this in the last war."

"That's my father's pistol from WWII. What war were you in?" Molly asked with interest.

"WWII," Eirian responded. Molly's mouth gaped. Eirian smiled at her demurely.

Molly harrumphed, reached back in her bag, and pulled out a most interesting-looking weapon. It was shorter and bulkier than a rifle. From the size of the barrel, it looked like a shotgun, but there was an extended metal brace attached to the front of the overlong pistol grip.

Molly pulled out four oversized ammo drums along with a smaller, camouflaged backpack, then stuffed three of the drums in the pack. The brace on the weapon's stock was a guiding mechanism locked the fourth drum in place beneath the barrel. We'd been regular shooting partners for years, so I knew she was well-heeled, but I'd never seen that particular weapon. I whistled, impressed.

Molly looked up to see us watching with interest. She hefted the weapon. "If civilization goes bye-bye, I will walk, talk, and sleep with this baby. It's my pride and joy; an AA12 auto-shotgun." Grinning with real joy, she said, "It can fire up to 300 twelve-gauge rounds per minute and is recoilless. A shotgun with a mouse's kick. Get it?" Patting the attached drum affectionately, she added, "These each hold twenty rounds, loaded with mid-to-close-quarters combat in mind."

Next, she pulled a thick camo-colored belt out of her bag, buckled it on, and slipped the Glocks into holsters on either hip. Extra clips lined the waistband. She reached into her bag one last time and handed two spare clips for each of their pistols to Smoke and Eirian. They thanked her, and Smoke opened his duster, shoving the Automag and clips into a wide leather belt already festooned with a pair of short axes and a sawed-off shotgun.

Everyone turned to look at me. I held up a hand, "Give me a sec."

I went back to the bedroom and eyed my knife where it lay on my nightstand, then buckled on an old tactical belt I used for the shooting range. Holstering my Colt, I did a quick touch-check on the pocketed clips, picked up my knife, and holstered it. The leather hilt felt comfortably warm to the touch, and I wondered where I'd had that thought before.

As I passed everyone, heading for the coat closet by the front door, I held up a finger and grinned. Reaching behind miscellaneous paraphernalia, I pulled out my shotgun. It was only a pump-action Mossberg, but it was my baby, and I was bringing it to the party.

Everyone was standing when I returned. I was tempted to share my dream with my friends, but Eirian had already laid a sheathed sword on the kitchen table. She said, "Molly, if you can fit it in with the arsenal you're carrying, I brought this blade for you." Molly unsheathed the rapier with an exclamation of delight and moved toward the conversation pit's far side to give it a try.

A smile tugged at one corner of my mouth. "Watch the furniture." Molly glanced back and stuck her tongue out. We all followed her into the front room. I knew she'd taken weapons training in her martial arts classes, and she swung the sword with a comfortable familiarity that left me a bit envious. If my dream sword had been real, I suspected it would be far more effective in her hands than mine.

I shook off the idle thought and looked around, considering our small company of warriors. We were well armed now. We had Plan A and a stab at Plan B. Jack the Ripper had brought evil to my city—with their help, we would exorcize his foul presence tonight. I said, "Molly, would you mind joining us." She came over, nodding her thanks to Eirian, a self-satisfied smile on her freckled face.

I bowed my head, praying over our weapons the same way I had the previous night. That ghostly light enveloped the piled arms again, and as the glow faded, I added a prayer for our safe return, then told the team,

"To get away from potential victims, we're heading out of town. I have a place in mind about twenty minutes from here. It's uninhabited at night and has the advantage of being surrounded by water."

Smoke and Eirian exchanged looks. "What?" I asked.

Smoke said, "Harmon Waite, water is anathema to demons and devils."

Eirian added, "Water is life. When it comes in contact with a servant of chaos, it shorts their powers.

I gnawed on that, then said, "I was only hoping to ensure containment, but we'll take any advantage we can get."

I ushered everyone out, locked up, and slid into the passenger side of Molly's cruiser. Molly put her tote and backpack in the trunk, then climbed into the driver's seat as Eirian and Smoke took up the back seat. She gave me a long, searching look, and I couldn't help but smile, enjoying the comfort of her presence. She relaxed, returned a slight smile, and turned the key in the ignition.

I took one last look over her shoulder at my little red brick house, then faced forward. The world is not an insecure place. My home, my city, my friends are what life is all about. Jack was an aberration. He belonged in Hell, not in our world. If we could not end him, we would send him back there—with finality.

Chapter 17 – Taking Down Jack

We headed out Highway 290, a well-traveled, four-lane thoroughfare. It stretches to Houston, but only ten miles on, we made a right and drove down the pockmarked asphalt of Decker Lane. Almost immediately, we arrived at Walter E. Long Lake's remote, water-locked geography—the place I'd chosen for our fight.

Parking in an empty lot that serviced a tallgrass prairie preserve where coyotes and, yeah, even prairie dogs roamed, we trekked through tall grasses. Enough evening lingered to make obstacles obvious, and Eirian ranged ahead, scouting for potential gates.

I closed my eyes, concentrated the light in my head, and let it spread outward until I felt the gentle brush of life-filled liquid slide into my perceptions. Awareness is a two-way street, and I opened my eyes long enough to ask, "Molly, while Eirian is searching, would you mind doing a visual reconnoiter of our immediate area?"

"Sure, Harmon," Molly responded, pleased to have something constructive to occupy her while we made like statues. I hummed happily, closed my eyes again, and refocused on the terrain. Close by, Smoke and Molly's auras throbbed with life, while Eirian's bright light moved steadily in the distance.

This extra sense revealed so much more than my eyes could. I drank it in like a blind man given sight. All those instances when paying attention to my instincts had saved my bacon flashed through my mind like a slideshow of lucky endings. I remembered what Gusion said, "If it is your will, and it is within your power, it will be. That is your gift from your father." Was he telling me I shared the angel's creation capabilities or was he talking about abilities like this?

I willed my God-light to reveal any gates, and at two places about equal distance from us, a hazy nimbus appeared above tall grasses. Only suggestions—scattered light being drawn like fireflies through windows between worlds—I understood both places to be potential portals. Still testing, I willed the others should see what I was seeing.

Smoke grunted, and Eirian's light started moving back in our direction. A good soldier, Molly kept to her perimeter sweep, but she looked my way, and I figured she caught some part of my sending. When Eirian arrived, her twinkling smile graced me with another delightful glimpse of her angel nature. "Harmon, I wonder what you will do for an encore."

I chuckled, "Wish I knew myself." I mulled over possibilities until Molly returned a few minutes later, reporting no hidden gullies, no animals close by, no surprises. My sight had already shown the few beasts roaming this preserve hunted closer to the peninsula's tip. There was one pack of coyotes, maybe a quarter-mile distant.

We took up our watch posts, Smoke and Eirian covering the northern gate, Molly and I facing south. I listened to the night while we sentineled. A delicate breeze sang its swishing lullaby among the high grasses. Crickets croaked their love songs, and an owl hooted its single sharp note of territoriality. It was nature's soothing ages-old rhythm. A soul-deep, Earth Mother's song. My worries sank into and were brushed to the periphery of my awareness by that timeless, tuneless melody.

Devils, demons, fallen angels, they had their plans, and the world was their playground. Still, our planet boasted an immense spirit that would endure much more than those minuscule beings could contrive. It would shrug off their machinations, even if we didn't.

A sudden energy spike jerked my head around. Five hellhounds bounded through the northernmost portal. A dozen of the diminutive, gremlin-like devils piled through after them. No Jack.

Dogs baying, Hell's minions following, they rushed in our direction. I gave Smoke a nod, appreciating his prescience, then pointed at the quiescent southern portal. "Ok, Jack's playing scaredy-cat. I'm going through that gate, and by God's good grace, I am dragging him into this world."

Molly gave me one hard look, then abruptly swung to stand shoulder to shoulder with the others. She didn't glance back but threw over her shoulder, "Be safe, or else."

I smiled with muted love into the empty space between us. Then, counting on my accelerated reality to take me to Jack and back to Earth before our team could be overwhelmed—with my first step—without conscious effort—I slowed time.

I didn't know how I was going to shove that oversized devil through a gate, but I willed it would be so. An instant before I arrived at the portal, I focused that same will on the potential of the southern gate and muttered, "Open sesame." I was through the portal before it finished shimmering into existence. Landing on Purgatory ground, I pivoted and raced toward a dark aura fouling the near horizon.

Jack was peering through the open doorway. Perhaps sensing my approach, he started to turn but was far too slow. I cushioned my body with light and slammed into the Ripper full speed. We both popped into my world, neat as you please. I pulled my knife instinctively as momentum rolled me through the tall grasses, then almost dropped it as my Ka-Bar lengthened into a full-sized sword. The blade Gusion had named Yeshu'a held to my palm, warming me with its living presence. I stood, and its thrumming hum filled the air.

Ugly, brutish, misshapen, a murderous mad beast, Jack keened in terror and scrabbled back. Even in my hyper-speed state, the living blade, gift of a fallen angel, blurred before my eyes. As though one—arm and sword slashed through a huge arcing swing—and Jack the Ripper's head parted from his neck as effortlessly as a hot knife slices through butter. The red gleam of his eyes radiated fear in the instant before his head went somersaulting through the air.

I didn't even stick around to watch it hit the ground. Pivoting, I was upon the hellspawn while the pack was still dozens of yards from my friends. Yeshu'a separated every evil creature's head from its shoulders before my brain could kick into gear and consider the absurd impossibility of what I was doing. Surrounded by drifts of dirty mist rising into the night sky,

Yeshu'a shivered once, radiating a sense of satisfaction, seemingly satiated by the destruction we had wrought.

Time slid back onto its track, and the shock on my teammate's faces came alive. Their weapons were still at the ready. They hadn't fired a single shot. "Damnation," Molly breathed.

Sword in one hand, pistol in the other, Eirian muttered, "What a waste of firepower." She glanced from her weapons to the blade in my hand that had seemingly appeared out of nowhere and gave me one of those heart-stopping smiles. "Neat encore, Harmon Waite. What about Jack?"

"Follow me," I said. Skirting shock, I shook myself back to normal with more effort than it had taken to kill Jack. Yeshu'a shrank into my old familiar knife again, exuding a contented aura as I slid it into the sheath on my belt. My whole team watched the process. Smoke grunted understanding, and Molly harrumphed. Eirian pursed her cupid lips but didn't say anything, just made a *let's get on with it* gesture.

As though avoiding an unholy place, we bypassed the massacre site and headed to the still-open northern gate. A flick of my will shut both it and its companion. We gathered around Jack's dismembered body, and Molly asked, "Why didn't Jack turn to smoke like the others?"

I heard the resolve in Eirian's voice, "Because a remnant of his power remains on this mortal plane." Molly took a step back. Eirian bestowed one of her smiles on Molly. I was pleased to see it affected her as much as it did me. "Don't worry. If we can gather enough firewood, I believe I can remedy that."

Smoke said, "That will not be necessary." He drew two matches out of a leather pouch attached to his belt. Placing one on Jack's body and the other on the separated head, he intoned a short prayer in his dissonantly melodic native tongue. The Ripper's remains erupted into flames. Smoke proclaimed with mischievous solemnity, "Sympathetic magic."

I swore I heard a howling scream in the distance, maybe from as far away as Hell. In mere moments fire immolated the body parts, and Jack's ashes drifted into the darkness of the night. I listened with quiet satisfaction as the Earth renewed its subtle symphony. The Moon, a pale maiden, slipped delicately above the horizon. In the distance, coyotes howled, and the air tasted dryly of coming winter. The rage that had filled me since Jenny's death drained into satisfaction.

I looked around at my team and felt a bit bad about stealing the show, but in my heart, I was relieved. They were safe. No one seemed very put out about missing a fight with devils and hellhounds. Their auras radiated the same content as my own. The book of our lives was still open, and I expected we had many more memories to make, but I was pleased to have finished the chapters belonging to Jack the Ripper.

I wrapped my silvery God-light around us to ease our return to Molly's cruiser. On the way, I felt a familiar presence. Riding on the ebbing tide of Jack's evil, perhaps drawn to our lights, Jenny's spirit had washed ashore near us. Smoke and Eirian saw her too. We all stopped, and I called to her. Jenny's ghost drifted our way, becoming more defined as its slender attention focused on us.

I heard Molly gasp. Smoke laid his big hand on my shoulder, called forth a tunnel of light, and murmured a prayer of closure for departing souls. Her pale shade diverted to and through that portal's promise, but at the last moment, Jenny turned and blessed me with a lingering ghost of her mischievous smile.

For the balance of our trip back, no one said a word. A quiet reverence for the universe's workings hung in the night air. We had only just arrived at the parking lot when the fallen angel appeared.

Chapter 18 – Smoke's Journey

He was hanging in the air over Molly's cruiser. An utterly beautiful being, he still seemed wretchedly wrong, an eons-twisted reminder that angels were God's first creation—an almost unbearably exquisite creature who had been born in Heaven but had chosen Hell.

Where Gusion had been a breath of summer, this angel was an ebony-marbled David come to life. He gazed down upon our poor team, his remorseless, implacable anger a tidal wave that overwhelmed. Molly went down to her knees. With growing foreboding, I stepped in front of her and asked as politely as possible, "Angel, please grant us your name.

His eyes were liquid gold. They heated at my careful question. "I am Yeqon. Uraqiel, the one you call Jack, is my creation, my child. He was also my pride—a terrible and mighty son. Now, his shadow cowers in Hell and gibbers of a human who cruelly robbed him of his pleasures, mortally crippled him, and stole his power to manifest on your dense plane."

Yeqon pointed, and the world dropped out from under me. The dark grip of his massive awareness wrapped my soul in a suffocating embrace. Dimly, I heard him continue, "You burned him, maimed him, made him small. You will answer for your crimes against my child."

My body was chained to his malice. My brain demanded I drop and grovel in front of his divine power. I would not. With great effort, I wrenched my head to one side and saw Eirian and Smoke. Their eyes were wild, but I could sense them straining against the shackles of Yeqon's will.

Behind me, Molly's sobs were heart-wrenching. With no protection, his celestial malevolence was shaking her world. I sent a prayer of comfort to her and heard her gasp in surprise. Her sobs gave way to snuffling tears. Yeqon noticed. "Harmon Waite, your friends mean much to you. Since they share the blame for Uraqiel's plight, I will entertain myself with their pain."

Reality shifted.

I was a ghost hanging above dirty, hard-packed snow. An Indian child knelt before a woman lying on the frozen ground. Nine, maybe ten years old, he shook her gently. He tried for a long time, but she never responded. Finally, an elderly woman, thin and frail, shuffled over and took the unmoving woman's right hand. Then she began to wail.

The boy stopped shaking the corpse I now knew was his mother's. He gazed up at the old woman, his face confused, frightened, tears running down his cheeks. As I watched, a sense of familiarity crept over me. I knew the giant of a man that child would become. It was Smoke, or at least a memory of Smoke's the angel had brought to life. I wondered if Smoke was living inside that memory or if he and the others were seeing the scene as I did.

I peered up and around. There was a river, not twenty yards distant. It was at least as impressive as our own Colorado. It was the same dismal hue as the leaden dawn with chunks of ice bobbing turgidly on its sluggish current. In the camp surrounding my ghostly presence, what must have been thousands or tens of thousands of Native Americans huddled together under thin blankets or slept on the snow.

They looked as miserable as human beings could—only slightly less gaunt than photos I'd seen of Nazi stalag survivors. That they were prisoners was evident by the campfires of Army guards circling the otherwise unshackled Indians along a broad, encompassing perimeter.

The soldiers were busy eating a hot breakfast. By their weapons and clothing, I guessed it was somewhere in the early 1800s. Not one of the Indians I could see had been given food. There was no grumbling among the prisoners, though. Only the coughs of the ill, which were everywhere, disturbed the muffled misery of that cruel winter morning. The same hopeless look burdened every man, woman, and child's eye.

At some point, an old man threw a blanket over the grandmother's shoulders and another over Smoke's. Lost in grief, neither noticed. Eventually, three young braves arrived. They wrapped his mother's body in a blanket, lifted her to their shoulders, and carried her south, skirting the river bank. As they hobbled after the men, Smoke supported the old woman, who must have been the grandmother who raised him.

Disembodied but tied to Smoke by Yeqon's will, I drifted along behind.

The braves arrived at the boundary of the encampment. Just beyond, perhaps a dozen corpses were piled on a makeshift bier. Other Indians were steadily wading through the dense grasses, laying stones on the dead, then moving off in search of more. The three men gently lowered his mother's corpse onto the pile. Smoke and his grandmother stood without moving until her body was covered by stones. The grandmother was impassive now. Tears streaked Smoke's face, but he didn't make a sound. The braves carried five more bodies to the pile in the next hour. The others did not complain. They just kept bringing rocks.

A group of soldiers assigned to oversee this makeshift burial of the night's dead was sitting or standing off to one side—far enough to avoid the rising stench. Most were smoking or chewing tobacco. Some looked sorry for the Indians. Others looked hard and callous. The weight of the dead sat on all, though. No one spoke.

While the bodies were being covered, other soldiers herded prisoners onto a large barge moored at the river's edge. A thick rope ran across the breadth of the river. I could see it was tied to a team of mules on the other side. When the raft was full, the mules hauled the clumsy craft toward the far bank. Two burly men stood on the upriver side of the barge. Each held a long staff with a steel hook on one end. Whenever a fragment of ice floated up against the barge, they hooked, then shoved it to the side so it could move downriver. They were kept busy for the best part of an hour until the barge reached the far shore.

When it returned, the army herded more Indians on board. Then, a wagon with four white people in it arrived. The Indians were forced back off the barge so the white folk could get across the river without being near any prisoners. When the barge returned the second time, the Indians were hustled on board again.

By gestures, one of the soldiers overseeing the burial made Smoke and his grandmother understand they were to get on the barge. As they were pulled across the wide river, I floated behind the craft, gazing down upon the half-frozen current. Although I was hanging above what would have been certain death for my body, my spirit hardly noticed. My thoughts were consumed by the immense tragedy I witnessed. The entire trip, Smoke stared back at the pile of rocks where his mother's remains were buried. When my ghost drifted across his sad gaze, I thought I caught a momentary glint of gold but couldn't be sure.

I contemplated the utter horror and misery of that place. I could not shed tears but felt my heart shredded by the suffering. Once we reached the far shore, I gazed around at the thousands more who sat desolately on that bank. I guessed they would be there until all the prisoners were ferried across the river. That would take days, with the slow process grinding to a halt every time a white passed blithely by on that trail of tears. For that was the only thing it could be. I thought it was the saddest sight I'd ever seen…

…until reality shifted again…

Chapter 19 – Eirian in the City of the Damned

E irian's silver mane was cut boyishly short and covered by a cavalier's hat that sported a single jaunty feather. I recognized it as a musketeer's outfit. I figured she was masquerading as a man since there wasn't much room for sword-wielding lasses back in—what was it—the fifteenth or sixteenth century.

She had a rapier with an elaborate guard held loosely in her right hand and carried a small child of maybe two or three in the crook of her left arm. Her blue eyes were so dark, they appeared black. A layer of grime marred the charm of her heart-shaped face.

Two slightly older boys each held a hand of the musketeers flanking her. All the musketeers had their swords drawn. The youngsters were finely dressed and huddled fearfully close to their guardians as the group moved warily through crooked, soot-shrouded streets.

Here and there, they came upon piles of stacked bodies. All the corpses were riddled with lesions. I realized they were making their way through a city consumed by the black plague. It had to be old London. One of my history books had covered the details. It was a significant infestation that killed roughly a quarter of the population in the 1600s, so that fit.

Their little party gave the stacked corpses as wide a berth as possible, considering the cramped streets. The two boys shrunk into their guides every time they passed one of the piles of rotting bodies. I remembered carts would come by to pick up the cadavers, but it looked like they were having problems keeping up with what, if they were near the height of the plague, had to have been several hundred new corpses a day.

I was only a ghost on the scene, but I could almost feel the musketeer's ratcheting fear. Back then, no one knew what caused the plague, and—prayer or invocation—I could not help the words that rose to my lips, "Even though I walk through the valley of the shadow of death, I will fear no evil, for you are with me."

A young girl appeared in the dimness of an open doorway. A nightmare of lesions covered her body. No more than five, she was obviously cared for. She was clean, her wounds smeared with a pasty remedy. She saw the children and came toward them. Eirian said something in old English I didn't quite catch, but the little girl only stopped when Eirian raised the point of her sword to the breast of her ragged linen shift. A woman came out of the doorway on the heels of the child. She was plainly the mother and looked in even worse shape—stumblingly close to death.

The woman put her hands on the little girl's shoulders—I thought to pull her back from the danger—but unmoving, her gaze bore deep into Eirian's. The distance between life and death passed between them in an instant. Eirian blinked once, then the woman shoved her child full onto the blade.

Eirian's sword ran through the little girl's heart and out her back. The child gave a single choked scream, then her frail frame slumped to the ground, sliding off the blade held nerveless in Eirian's hand. The Nephilim's eyes turned a stormy purple—shock, horror, and immense anger flashing through them in rapid succession. She looked like she wanted to run the mother through. I saw her mouth one word, "Why?"

The other musketeers stepped back with their charges. The two boys stared at the fallen form of the little girl. Comprehension dawned, and both began to cry. The mother did not respond to Eirian's question. She paid no further attention to the group, but gathered her daughter's limp body in her arms, leaned against the wall, and fell into a makeshift cradle around the slight form. She held her daughter in her lesion-covered arms, and a rain of tears fell upon the child's still face.

One of the musketeers said something. Eirian didn't move, just stared. She had unwittingly murdered an innocent, and I knew it had shaken her angel's soul. The man spoke again more urgently. Eirian started, tightened her grip on the toddler in her charge, looked back at the other two musketeers, then started moving on down the street without looking back at the woman or the child.

As my disembodied ghost was pulled after them, I floated tearless past the two motionless figures. They were huddled, one just this side, the other beyond death's door—the mother almost as far from life as the daughter. I did not believe she would ever move again. She had saved her child from dying after her but would join her soon. I muttered words, unbidden and unheard, "Holy Mary, pray for them. Saint Joseph, pray for them. Jesus, Mary, and Joseph assist them beyond their last agony."

Then, with an effort of absolute anguished, outraged will, I pulled myself out of Eirian's memories. Surprise darkened the fallen angel's face. The rest of my team were on their knees, tears streaming down their faces. I felt my own tears as I turned to Yeqon, an inexorable tide of anger overwhelming my heart. What I had to say to him, I felt compelled to say, "God, who created you, is no longer with you. The name, Yeqon, that He gave you is dead. I name you Evil, and that is the only name will have meaning from now to the end of time."

I expected to be blasted on the spot. Instead, the fallen angel ignored me and fixed his attention on Molly. When his eyes flickered back toward mine, a cruel smile touched the corners of his perfect lips. I knew he had decided what to do about my puny judgment. In that smile was all the malevolence of his twisted eons. There was no hint, no trace of an angelic being in front of me. The fathering of two-hundred Grigori devils had twisted his angel's heart into ruin.

No longer even a fallen angel, what remained of this creature was only a manifestation of cruel power. His existence was beyond pity. He was a travesty of creation, a fragment of Hell that had no place in our world. Yet, he dared to leave that abandoned place and come here to my Earth to destroy the ones I loved. As he focused intently on Molly, I felt his power rise, and his purpose radiated like a shock wave through my soul—this fallen angel knew what had happened to me and how I had escaped!

He intended to take Molly on a similar journey through Hell, but escape would not happen for her. I realized my palm wrapped my naked blade, and Yeshu'a was growing, his anticipation warming my hand. I lunged forward and drove my blessed blade through that fallen angel's black heart.

In rapid succession, Yeqon expressed shock, contempt, anger, and finally, puzzlement. One arm rose to point at me accusingly. I could feel Yeshu'a absorbing his eternal presence into its steel embrace as a wave of wild power erupted from Yeqon's fading form. The metal heart of my blade swelled, and my conscious mind crumbled, ripped to pieces by celestial waves of destructive energy. I had no chance to defend myself.

There was only time for a single thought.

Light spread through me, protecting me. A feeling beyond power laid soothing hands on my shredding soul. I was embraced by love—the fragments of my blasted spirit consecrated and made well again. Healed and filled with the wholeness of life, I knew the rightness that exults in every fiber of every being under creation. I was the Universe. I was me. The power of light and life comforted, held safe, and blessed my self as one with the whole, but still one. Still me.

When conscious thought returned, I looked down, and my blade was just a blade. I reached up and ran a hand over my face in wonder. I had tasted a loving perfection I knew I would never forget. The fallen angel was gone. For a single blessed instant, the night was peaceful again.

Then I felt a gate activate. I looked and saw a horde of giant devils pouring into our world.

Chapter 20 – Battle with a Bunch of Jacks

It wasn't two hundred Grigori, probably more like twenty, but that was a couple dozen Jacks, a much scarier sight than an entire swarm of hounds and minions. Big, ugly, and coming through the southmost gate, they were hardly more than a long football throw from our parking lot. I wondered if they had been waiting on their father's word to give us one final, terminal surprise after he finished playing with us. Now they were a pack of first-generation devils, with all the strength that implied, charging us with vengeance in their eyes and murder in their hearts.

My team was already up and shaking off the horror of their experiences. I coughed diplomatically, pointed at the devils, and said, "Looks like y'all get a chance to use your weapons after all."

I moved to help Molly up as Smoke and Eirian locked and loaded. Smoke looked like he was still wrapped in winter's cold. Eirian appeared more like an avenging angel. It was the first time I'd seen her angry. I found it both terrifying and reassuring. I gave Molly a quick hug. She looked from me to our teammates, then her eyes widened as she followed their gazes and saw the onrushing spawn of a fallen angel's creation schemes. Tails, horns, hoofs, and other animal traits told me more than I wanted to know about how Yeqon created and incubated his offspring.

My time sense kicked in. I traveled thirty paces to my right, then held Yeshu'a poised and ready. My blade screamed, a high, piercing, metallic cry of mad joy. Devil heads snapped around at the sound, and half the pack split in my direction. That was fine by me. I smiled grimly and waited—out of my team's line of fire. When the first monster reached me, my blade and I blurred past in perfect harmony, and a tusked, bewildered head tumbled away—while the grotesque body fell in slow motion.

Then, the gang of devils was upon me. Even with time on my side, I didn't dare stand to meet them. I darted right and took two strides forward to lop the head off a gargoyle-faced devil still focused on where I had been. I missed seeing the clawed hand coming in under the high arc of my sword and had to dance away from a searing pain in my side. I swung back toward a black-maned devil with a mouth full of teeth and huge bone-tipped paws, then stepped with savage satisfaction into the full singing swing that sheared his head off.

I blurred forward, and two twitching bodies lay between the remaining pack and my hungry, happy sword. A devil with cracked grey rhino hide and a wide, smashed nose leaped over the corpses. Panic flared to life in his burning eyes just before Yeshu'a sliced cleanly through his thick, corded neck.

A tall, shaggy devil, part mad angel, part ape, or perhaps Sasquatch, kicked that falling body out of the way. Before he could take another step, Yeshu'a drove through his heart. I dodged his swipe but had to leave the blade in his chest. It continued singing its wordless song in a high, keening voice as the Yeti-sized fiend stumbled back.

Seeing me bladeless, the Grigori piled on from every side, and I went down under their combined weight—tooth and claw seeking my flesh.

It was the strangest thing. Even amid my peril, in the hyper-speed heat of battle, my brain noted when the fast, booming rhythm of Molly's auto-shotgun ceased. Instinctively, I willed a blast of purest white light. It exploded outward, and the weight of devils shriveled to ash.

I tangentially realized I had gone with the nuclear option as I rolled, snatched up Yeshu'a, and started running toward the gate—following a big beast of a devil who had Molly tucked under one arm. She was struggling to bring her shotgun around. The devil noticed what she was doing and, seizing the AA12 with his free hand, crushed it like paper.

I screamed a single, desperate mental command, Molly, shut your eyes and keep them shut! They disappeared through the gate, and adrenaline shot me into Purgatory in time to see their shadowed forms vanish through a second shimmering portal. I'd already known where they were headed. His children must be bound to their father's desires because this devil was going to fulfill them.

I hurtled the gap in a single bound and landed in Hell again, removing that sorry devil's head, grabbing Molly, pressing her face to my chest, and leaping back through the gate—all in that time-sped motion made reality flow like glue. I could only hope she hadn't seen what I had way too much time to take in—another level of Hell, far more horrible than the chambers I'd witnessed previously. My single sight of its abominations was almost too reason-blasting, bat-shit insane to comprehend.

I fell back through the gate, Molly still cradled to my chest. She gripped me as tightly as I held her, eyes tight shut. Her pain and fear brought me back to my senses. I stepped through the Purgatory portal into the Austin night, Molly a precious burden—balm for heart and mind.

I could see Smoke and Eirian, still fighting. Another Sasquatch-looking devil, as large as Smoke himself, was behind the Indian with an arm around his throat. Smoke was dragging the hairy beast around the paved area while he took chunks out of other devils with his twin axes.

Eirian was a master swordswoman at work, a blur of speed in the dim light. I saw her whirl behind Smoke, and her sword flashed. The Yeti-looking monster on Smoke's back screamed but didn't let go. Molly was still in my arms, but as the sounds of combat drifted to us, she looked around and shoved against my chest, "Put me down, Harmon. Go help your friends."

My friend's spirit brought me a healing grin, and I lunged into hyper-speed, her weight not slowing me one bit. A few real-time seconds later, I set Molly on her feet at the edge of the parking lot. She gasped, "What a rush," then drew both pistols and commenced picking targets as she moved purposefully toward the fray.

I crossed the parking lot and beheaded the devil on Smoke's back. Yeshu'a sang his battle song in hyper-time, and I wondered what the others were hearing.

Even as I fought, the hellish scene I'd just witnessed lurked like a waking nightmare. What I'd seen in that chamber pushed me beyond anger. No matter how evil they'd been in their short lives, those condemned souls endured eternal torments far beyond righteous retribution.

The white heat of my God-light consumed me. I'd had enough of Hell. A broad horizontal sweep of my blade mentally swept my world free of evil—burning every devil there, moving or not, to ash.

Chapter 21 – Prelude to War

We headed back to my place. Eirian helped me whip up enough bacon, eggs, and toast to satisfy even Smoke. Too tired to drive, Smoke and Eirian crashed on my conversation pit. Molly came to bed with me, but there was nothing sexual in how she held me as she fell into a troubled sleep.

Molly had heard my mental shout and kept her eyes closed in those few instants, thank God. As tough as she was, I knew she needed the safety of friendly arms to re-anchor a reality that did not include visits to Hell.

What was it I saw in that chamber? That I will not share. Hell is always worse than you can imagine. I pray you live a good life and let it remain that way.

Before dropping off to sleep myself, I placed a call to Noble. I told him his daughter's murderer was dead, and I'd head out there in a few hours to report in detail.

Smoke and Eirian had left by the time we awoke. I dropped Molly off at her house in Tarrytown. She was still groggy, but the shadows were more under her eyes than in them. I promised to bring her back to her cruiser upon demand.

At the front door of his mansion, Noble greeted me with a bear hug. We sat in his living room, and I focused on the view out his oversized windows while I sorted my thoughts. Noble waited on me. I knew what he wanted. My explanations to date had held little water. Was I going to tell him what had been going on? There was really no choice. I recounted everything just as it had happened. He'd either believe me or not.

Of course, that meant telling him I'm an angel's son. While I talked, he kept his eyes on my face. They were not disbelieving. Hungry might have been a better word. When I finished, Noble stared at his hands in his lap, then turned them over and studied his palms.

When he looked back up, there was a hint of the old steel in his eyes. "Harmon, I first noticed something was different about you when I watched you play football. You had catches that were absolute perfection. I couldn't have scripted them any better."

He was quiet for a bit, then admitted, "I got ahold of the game films, played them back in slow motion, and saw something extraordinary. A moment when, not the camera, but you, Harmon Waite, actually blurred on film. You'd be one step late to the ball, then you'd just be there, football in hand and, like in that game against the Sooners, headed for their goal line, slipping past those Oklahoma players slicker than a greased hog."

I winced. "Noble, I didn't know who or what I was back then. I did know I was more than lucky, but my youth got in the way, and I just enjoyed the cheers. My seeming ability to slip through time only happens in extreme situations. When I thought about it back then, I wrote it off as adrenaline. Figured what I was doing wasn't as crazy as it felt."

Noble eyed me shrewdly. "Son, I knew it wasn't humanly possible for someone to move so fast the camera couldn't catch it, but I left it alone. After all, why kill the golden goose? I figured somebody else would see what I'd seen sooner or later. But, either no one noticed, or more likely, didn't believe what they saw. Then you got hurt bad and were gone to the army."

"When you came back, you decided to be a detective. I threw a few tough cases your way and kept tabs on the results. What Morrow told me only confirmed your ability to do extraordinary things. I don't doubt a bit of what you've told me, and if Jenny's death put you on the track of something that evil, then there is at least the hope of meaning there. That doesn't help much, but it does help."

He stared at his hands again, sighed, and finally admitted, "I don't know what to do with myself, but I believe in purpose. Our entire civilization is built on the bones of persistence. Nothing else matters."

That sounded like the old Noble. Unwilling to break the mood, I simply nodded in agreement. Noble looked me up and down, taking my measure. "Harmon, I know you wouldn't have let me do this, so I paid off your mortgage today. I don't want to hear any backtalk, either. I'm an old man. I got no other family and nothing else to do with my money now that Jenny's gone. I don't want you to have to worry about house payments while you're out there doing this old world the kind of good you've done for me."

I realized my mouth was open when he grinned at me. I shut it and thanked him. Not much else I could do. Noble looked suddenly more intent, and I realized he wasn't done. "Son, it sounds like you got some good people around you now. The hardest thing to find in this world is an A-team—people you can trust to do what is needed when it is needed. I don't want to see them scatter now that you've taken care of that devil, Jack."

Noble paused, his blue eyes sharpening—radiating a nearly electric intent. This was the Noble who'd built an empire. He wanted something and was closing in for the kill. "You do know it's not over, don't you."

He caught me completely by surprise. "What's not over?"

"Think about it. From what you're telling me, there's a war going on. You just put a whupping on the other side. They'll be coming after you. Don't let 'em surprise you, and don't be alone when they get here."

I shifted uncomfortably but knew he was telling the truth. I just hadn't thought it through. The idea of Hell coming after me was daunting. The thought that it might come after my friends too, well, that got my dander up. Noble had been observing me like a hunting tiger. Now he pounced, "You know, I can help."

That old man was two steps ahead, and I struggled to catch up. "Noble, I appreciate what you're saying. I even agree. But if I have a target on my back, you should be keeping your distance, not offering to help."

Noble snorted, "Like hell, I will! Harmon, I call you son for a reason. I have the resources to be useful to you. You are in this fix because of me.

Don't think I'm not gonna help, and it ain't just weapons I'm talking about. Having a handle on what's going on in the world around you may help you see 'em coming. I can provide that intelligence. I tell you, I will help!"

He had me at a disadvantage now, and there was something alien, almost like pleading, in his arctic blue eyes. He threw down the gauntlet. "Whether you like it or not, you will give me something useful to do in my old age."

For a long, silent moment, we stared at each other. Noble had lost his only child. I could see him struggling to rebuild his world. Finally, I put out my hand. "I don't know if the others will stick around, so it may be a very small one, but welcome to the team, sir. And—thank you."

Noble took my hand, squeezing it with surprising strength. I could see plans in his eyes, and I had to admit I felt a certain comfort knowing I had such a powerful ally on whatever kind of team I had just committed to keeping together. My concerns were background noise that would likely come out and muster for inspection on the way home.

What did the future bring? I couldn't know, but Noble had convinced me of one thing—my quiet days with only a good paperback for company were likely behind me. My drive back was indeed filled with doubts, but when I walked in the door of my mortgage-free little red brick home, there was a sense of security and freedom in those four walls that hadn't been there when I left.

Almost as soon as I got home, my phone rang. Molly wanted her car back. I played taxi and enjoyed the look on her face when I told her what Noble had done. She was pleased for me, and we had to stop for a celebratory drink. Over the next few weeks, our friendship tiptoed back into its normal rhythms. I did share everything Noble had said—and getting prepared for a showdown neither of us was sure of proved to be an interesting new topic of conversation.

Eirian dropped by my office that next afternoon. I asked, and she told me she'd found my business in the white pages. She let me know Noble had offered her Jenny's furnished condo. His only request was that Eirian pack up Jenny's belongings. He said it was too painful for him to do. He also told her to keep anything she liked.

Noble had said he wanted her to hang around and get a different take on his city. Of course, he didn't know about her previous visit. She accepted because, as she told me, "I need to teach you a bit more about your powers, particularly how to properly wield your imposing blade. Did you know Yeshu'a means Deliverance in Hebrew?"

"Yeah, I looked it up," I said. I told Eirian about my dream in detail, then added, "I don't know if I trust it to that extent because of who made it, but I expect that blade is as much a part of me as it is of Gusion."

The next time I saw Noble, he mentioned he'd also tried to do something nice for Molly, but she wouldn't accept a gift from him. It was a police thing. I recounted how she'd lost her AA12 during the final fight. A few days later, Molly dropped by my office. While visiting, she admitted Noble had presented her with a new AA12 and a half dozen ammunition drums. She was excited because the weapon had been redesigned with a gas recoil that let her put on a whupping with even greater ease. With a smug smile, she claimed it was also cooler looking than the old one.

Noble had told her if any devils showed up in Austin in the future, he wanted her suitably armed, so she kept the weapon. "After all, Harmon," she told me, "It's no kind of bribe, just your employer making good on your expenses." I teased her a bit, but was happy she had her *hell and high water* protection back.

Smoke and I had gone out for drinks a couple times already, but the big Indian showed up at my door at the break of dawn two Saturdays after our fight with Yeqon and his children.

He was stoic about rousting me out of a sound sleep, but I got that he wanted me to go somewhere with him. He'd brought coffee and a sack of bacon, egg, and cheese biscuits from McDonald's, so I held my tongue. Of course, he consumed most of the food while I was in the shower. I ate the last biscuit and finished a coffee before we headed out my front door.

Smoke's blue Hudson Hornet was at the curb—a new boat hitched to the back. Bold black letters on its bow read *Pursuit*. It had a canopy-covered wheelhouse and a Honda outboard engine attached to the stern. Next to the engine, a luxuriously oversized ice chest was bungied to a wide shelf that hung off the aft end.

I teased him, "Smoke, I didn't know you were rich."

Smoke looked a bit embarrassed. "Harmon Waite, because I helped you find his daughter's killer, your friend Noble Summers searched me out and demanded he be allowed to do something for me. He told me to choose anything up to and including a new house. I told him I could use a fishing boat. I was thinking of something more modest, but this showed up yesterday. I am not an Indian-giver, so here I am."

He did the Spock thing with his left eyebrow, and I couldn't help laughing. "No, Smoke, I don't guess you could do anything but accept it. You probably made Noble very happy." I rubbed the stubble on my jaw as I looked at his new, monster-sized fishing rig. "You know this thing belongs on the ocean, not in a river."

"Ok, Harmon Waite. Let's go to Galveston and give it a proper christening."

I gave him the fisheye, then gave his brand-new craft the once over again. It wasn't hard to make up my mind. "Let me grab an overnight duffel, and I'll be right with you." Smoke's smile was angelic.

Waite on the Blind Angel – The Celestial Wars Book Two - The Monster Trap

Out in the rolling hill country, a giant figure rose out of a still-smoking crater. Nearly thirty feet tall, it was encased in a black suit of armor that glowed redly from the heat of its journey between worlds. The figure held a massive longsword openly in its gloved right hand. For a time, it stood like stone, gazing into the sky. Then it turned to face north and began a long but relentlessly steady journey toward the city of Austin. As it walked, its form shimmered, then disappeared from view.

Out on Lake Travis, a mountain of a man, a Cherokee Indian named Smoke on Distant Mountain, the son of the son of an angel, with ancient eyes and a long, bold nose set in a craggy face, sat fishing below the west-most dam. His boat was top-notch, a well-rigged vessel that would have been at home on the ocean. He was reeling a catfish up from the depths when he suddenly paused. The fish struggled uselessly against his strength while he stared south, listening to some inner prompt. Long moments passed. Then he shook himself, finished reeling in the fish, dropped it in an over-large ice chest strapped to the back of the craft, started the motor, and headed directly toward the dock where his big sedan was parked.

He backed his car onto the concrete ramp and loaded his boat onto the trailer with unhurried efficiency. Then he pulled a pair of tomahawk axes out of his trunk and laid them on the front seat. Exiting the parking lot, he pointed the nose of his blue monster of a car, a Hudson Hornet he'd proudly owned since 1952, south along Highway 620.

Following the curving highway, Smoke hugged the western shoreline of Lake Travis, continued past the retired-rich-enough community of Lakeway, then turned right onto Bee Cave Road. A few miles later, he swung right again to merge onto Highway 71. That highway cut a diagonal line through what had been a limestone seabed two-hundred and sixty million years ago. Sometime after the water receded, tectonic forces buckled the limestone upward into the modern hill country landscape, with its wave upon wave of rolling hills.

Periodically glancing to his left, Smoke continued along 71 for about eight miles. He came to a flyspeck of a town called Spicewood, took a long, hard look down a narrow country road with a roadsign read Reimers–Peacock, turned left, and followed the pavement until the concrete ran out. He kept the big car bouncing along the dirt for several more miles until he finally stopped and climbed out, axes in hand.

He stood squinting into the distance, paying close attention to the strength of what he felt. Then he leaned back against the door of his sedan. Axes held comfortably in crossed arms, he remained relaxed but ready. For almost an hour, he waited serenely, as unmoving as the mountain he resembled. Then tension crept with a slow grind over his massive frame. His eyes narrowed to slits, and he stood away from his vehicle, uncrossing his arms. The landscape remained utterly still and empty.

Smoke began circling to his left, using the shadows under the tall oaks to mask his own presence. His eyes, all this time fixed south, began tracking east as he kept his face turned toward the evil he sensed. He charged with a sudden mighty war cry and threw the ax in his right hand. The head clanged loudly as it bounced off a giant black form that shimmered into, then immediately back out of sight.

Running full speed toward where he'd seen the enormous figure, Smoke suddenly threw himself to the ground and skidded on his stomach, rocks scraping his elbows. He rolled sideways and was up again, backpedaling furiously. The giant flickered into view—the sword Smoke had somehow avoided swinging back to the ready. Smoke threw his other ax. It too clanged off the armor, doing no damage.

For a moment, the two giants stood poised, appraising each other, then a red beam appeared in the armored figure's visor. Smoke turned and ran, long, leaping strides that put him back among the trees. An intense humming filled the air, and a narrow beam of light shot out from the helmet's visor. It hit a gnarly old oak Smoke had ducked behind, and the shockwave from the exploding tree threw the big Indian off his feet.

Dazed but still aware, Smoke levered himself off the ground. Directly between him and where the black armored figure had stood, the splintered base of a tree remained. After swatting him, the monster evidently forgot about Smoke and resumed its journey toward Austin. The angel's grandchild moved out of the trees and peered northwest, where he could still sense the creature's ancient aura. He pondered the situation.

It didn't take him long to decide he needed heavier weaponry and reinforcements. Smoke climbed back into his Hudson, found an open enough spot to make a wide turn, and headed back toward the highway. He glanced over when he felt himself drawing even with the creature, but he didn't expect to see anything through the trees. The wooded countryside looked undisturbed, but Smoke calculated the direction and thought the city of Austin might be in trouble. Yeah, his teammates would want to know about this ASAP.

About Author

Written by John C. Campbell

Narrated by Daniel C. Johnson

Dan Johnson's performances really bring these stories to life. The audio version of Chapter One "The Murder of Jenny Summers," plus the story behind this revised edition can be found @ www.thecreativenow.com/evolved-content.

Please take a moment to leave a review. They help keep this series going and to be honest, I get a big kick out of reading them. Most relevant review links are gathered @ www.thecreativenow.com/reviews-links.

In addition to member-only content, discounts, and giveaways, The Creative Now's monthly newsletter helps you keep up with Harmon Waite's ever-escalating adventures in *The Celestial Wars*. You can sign up at www.thecreativenow.com/subscription. Your sign-up bonus includes multiple free short stories set in Harmon's universe—all performed by "The Celestial Wars" series narrator, Dan Johnson.

If you want to say hello, have questions, or would like to join my arc team, please email me @ john.campbell@thecreativenow.com.